2
0
2
4

2
0
2
4

H. Berkeley Rourke

Let your plans be dark and impenetrable as night.
When you move, fall like a thunderbolt.
Sun Tzu, The Art of War

The Beginning

The day it began, a Tuesday, in San Francisco, was cloudy, a little foggy, clammy, depressing to many. The day it began in Phoenix it was 105 degrees, air conditioners were running full capacity, people were running from malls to their cars to avoid the heat, starting their cars remotely with the air conditioning running if they had that capacity, waiting in the car with open windows as the cooling began if they did not have that capacity. The day it began in Miami, Florida there was a downpour early in the morning from a localized thunderstorm that went out to sea nearly as quickly as the rain stopped falling, leaving a partially cloudy day that was warm, humid, and getting warmer as it went along.

In Moscow, Russia, the day it began there was a beautiful bright day in progress, but there was some fear as well because the press was so preoccupied with the difficulties in the Ukraine that had been going on for years. In Beijing, China, a new moment of crisis was occurring in the economy. Though the government had been increasingly allowing capitalist enterprises, many of them had failed leaving large numbers of the population without work, hungry and many even without housing. Those without housing had begun to move into the abandoned cities and buildings that came from the failures. And they were restive, uncontrolled in large measure despite the monolithic Chinese Army.

But all those places and most others on this great Mother Earth were much more peaceful in the ultimate moments than was Baghdad. For ten years the ISIS groups with various names had been warring with the government. For five years the Shia and the Sunni had warred with each other pretending to be warring about anything but religion. But the root, the actual basis for the war was their age old dispute over who should have taken the caliphate on Muhammed's death. And there were those on both sides that wanted to extend the caliphate to the entire world by whatever means could be used for accomplishment of that lofty goal.

For more than five years, the intensity of the war had grown while the rest of the world watched from afar. And for more than five years a small cabal of Shia had been paying for the acquisition and transport of a weapon, a weapon they thought would have consequence in the war, from Pakistan to the West where it ended up in Donetsk. The transaction had been highly secret and was known only to three men in the entire world, Abu Kalil Al Ghantrous, Falik Saleem, and Pasha Hashimi were the names of those three.

Even those who transported the weapon along with Falik did not know what they were carrying. It came in components that Falik had trained to assemble. When he and the two other men who transported the weapon to Donetsk arrived there he shot both of them in the head, dumped their bodies in a culvert well east of Donetsk and went on to the city. He assembled the weapon and engaged the very sophisticated timing device that would set it off on a Tuesday afternoon.

Hashimi was a Colonel in the ISI of the Pakistani Army. It was discovered by a subordinate that he was selling weapons to people in other countries. The subordinate wanted a cut of the profits. Hashimi refused the request and made plans to kill the man. But before he could do that, the man turned Hashimi in to the ISI. His interrogation was brutally intensive and physical; he was left with no fingers on his right hand. It would have been lopped off by a sword in time anyway, since he was declared a thief. His injuries, inflicted during the interrogation, caused his demise.

Hashimi confessed to many crimes, but his interrogators didn't have sufficient information to understand the largest and most dangerous of his crimes. Pasha had been able to sell one smallish nuclear weapon to the group in Iraq headed by Kalil. The group was known as the Sword of Fallujah. Its name derived from the city of Fallujah, of course. But it also came from the brother, Benji, that Kalil had lost to the Sunnis in the early battles there in the period of 2014-2018.

Kalil made arrangements for the weapon he purchased from Pasha to be delivered with Falik overseeing its transport, albeit by an extremely circuitous route, to Sevastopol, a port city on the coast of Crimea. From Sevastopol it was taken across the Crimea into Ukraine where it was placed in Donetsk. When Russia annexed Crimea in 2014 Kalil began to think of a way that he could entice the filthy infidels into war which might enable his group and groups like it to re-establish the caliphate throughout the central part of the Near East.

At the same time, Kalil purchased the nuclear weapon from Pasha at a cost of over $100,000,000.00, he also purchased a smaller but equally deadly weapon from a group of separatists in the deepest and most uninhabited jungles of Kenya. This weapon, somewhat unsophisticated in nature, but deadly as it could be contained a vial of Ebola virus. The virus held in the vial had proved to be aerosol borne in Kenya. It was encased in a simple explosive device which would rupture the tube of Ebola and let it free in the air at the moment desired by the user. The explosion causing this to occur would be no louder than a person passing gas. But it would be far deadlier to anyone within a short distance of the release of the virus.

All these things coalesced with the events in Ukraine leading to over a hundred dead Ukrainian soldiers and incursions into Ukrainian airspace by the Russian Air Force. Several air to air battles were fought between the older Sukhoi-30 fighter jets of the Ukrainian Air Force and the more advanced and capable Mig-39 jets of the Russian Air force, with predictable results. Just as it had occurred once before in Georgia, in Putin's first incursion into the states formerly constituting the Soviet Union, the outnumbered Ukrainian pilots were brave and capable but outgunned and out flown by the Russians.

The current state of affairs in Israel, always a source of unrest in the Middle East in general, was not much better. The Sunni forces in the ISIS groups and others of similar names had made very large inroads into Jordan. While there, they recruited thousands of new Jihadis from the camps. The desperate Alouites and Sunnis pushed out of Syria in the period prior to 2015, and who were among the Palestinians, also mostly Sunnis, had been spoiling for a fight with the "EESRAEELEES" for a long time. The swollen Sunni forces of ISIS, armed by Hezbollah, Hamas and by Assad of Syria, swarmed toward the Israeli border while the Russians began to occupy the eastern areas of Ukraine.

Of course the Israelis were not going to sit and do nothing while an invading army threatened their borders. For once the country of Jordan showed some military sense as well as political sense. Despite it having a majority of Sunni Muslims as its primary population, and when the Israelis made their initial, predictable air strike on the ISIS units, the Jordanians attacked with tanks and artillery as well. The result was much the same as the destruction of Saddam Hussein's army on the "Highway of Death." Thousands of the ISIS force died instantly in Hellfire missile attacks, artillery shelling and cluster bomb attacks launched by both the Israelis and the Jordanians.

The remaining members of the attacking force, seeing they were being destroyed in wholesale numbers, fled across the desert back into the friendly confines of Iraq and Syria. The Israelis, undaunted by the bellicose statements from Egypt, Syria and other nearby nations, including the fighting groups of Hezbollah, maintained their attack until literally thousands more died.

The Jordanians defended their borders and left the arena to the Israelis. Then the Jordanian Air Force began to sortie against the Israeli Air Force. It was not authorized initially by the government, but it happened and both Jordanian and Israeli jets went down. Jordan backed away instantly knowing it did not have the capability to fight an air war with the Israelis.

Then out of Syria a flight of nearly one hundred fighter/bomber aircraft, mostly Sukhoi 30's that had been purchased from the Russians, were spotted on a course that could only mean an attack on Israel. By the time all this happened the U.S. Sixth Fleet, the Mediterranean Sea Fleet maintained at all times, was about three hundred miles off the shore of the extreme northern part of Syria. It was closer yet to Lebanon. From several airports in Lebanon the fleet detected the firing of missiles which could only be directed at the ships of America. The missiles, all older and less stealthy or more capable of being dealt with by the fleet, were destroyed.

The fleet immediately went to a status of general quarters combat readiness. The runways of the airports in the eastern part of Lebanon that had launched the attack on the fleet were destroyed by cluster bombs dropped from cruise missiles fired from the protective cruisers surrounding the two nuclear powered aircraft carriers of the fleet. Aircraft were launched repeatedly and in staggered formations, time wise to protect the fleet. Some of the Syrian jets came too close to the fleet, and were destroyed without ado by the protective ring of FA-18 fighter planes that had been launched the minute the missiles were seen by the fleet.

The Jordanian Air Force saw the Syrian launch of aircraft toward Israel. But they did nothing. The Israeli Air Force was outnumbered initially but fought brilliantly and destroyed virtually the entire group of Sukhois. The Russians watched this from Sevastopol knowing that some of the Sukhoi pilots were their brethren. The Russians sent a group of Mig 39's southward, armed to the teeth. The Americans misunderstood. They shot down half the Mig fighters from long distance with missiles capable of being destructive at a distance of over a hundred miles from launch.

The remainder of the Israeli Air Force launched their fighters in the general direction the Russians were coming from. The Russians, when their planes started falling from the sky as a result of the missiles fired from FA-18 fighters, turned tail. But they too loosed their missiles. The result was several American and Israeli planes were lost as well.

Again the telephones between Washington, D.C. and Moscow were nearly worn out with the constant usage. Again the president tried to persuade Premier Putin the entire thing started as a result of ISIS attacking the Israelis. Putin, whose arms industry was making billions arming the Syrians, the ISIS groups as well as the Shia militias with more modern Russian weaponry, dismissed the assurances of the President and at one point even threatened to attack the Sixth Fleet as a result of the air battle in which all had lost assets.

Putin finally seemed to relent and back off his belligerence. The truth was he didn't think the Russian military was quite ready to engage the U.S. As was the U.S. military, the Russian military might was stretched a little thin as it sought to annex Ukraine with standby forces. It guarded its eastern borders with divisions devoted entirely to checking any Chinese incursions. It prepared constantly for the potential of nuclear war, preparing both offensively and defensively.

Kalil watched all these developments carefully, plotted his timing with great glee. He thought the Ebola virus a perfect response to all this. In an area of Crimea controlled by the Russians, where there were massed Russian troop formations near the Ukrainian border, the ebola was let loose. The effects were incredibly monstrous. Thousands of troops died of hemorrhagic fever. It was days before the nature of the fever was diagnosed properly. The small device had been carefully placed in a Russian encampment in Crimea.

Of course the Russians immediately blamed the Ukrainians, and then the Americans, in the press. But the real difficulty with the situation was the Russians blamed the Americans diplomatically. The Kremlin sent several messages to the President of the United States in outrage over the use of weapons of mass destruction which could only have been marshaled through the efforts of the United States. It was at the very least a frightening moment in history, a moment of great wonder from the American side. The Americans had no understanding of what could have happened. The Russian military was quite convinced the U.S. was responsible.

Letters flew back and forth from Washington, D.C. to Moscow. The president called Prime Minister Putin at least a dozen times to try and persuade him it was not the United States that had done this. Putin was adamant that President Hillary Clinton, the only woman president in the history of the United States of America, was responsible for the murder of thousands of Russian troops. President Clinton did everything she could to try and persuade Prime Minister Putin, the long time dictator of Russia, it was not true. He was unconvinced. More, he thought she was lying to him.

Russia, which had long been building new ICBM's, began to place units around the country on alert. These units were known to the U.S. in part but there were several new forces in the north central part of Russia holding concealed ICBMs capable of hitting the U.S. after flying over the North Pole.

Without a lot of publicity, the military of the United States quietly went from Defcon 1, basically a peacetime status, to Defcon 2. The anti-missile batteries that had been made into mobile units began to be placed surreptitiously in areas where warheads might pass overhead. The Navy began to maneuver its missile firing ships in ways that would present Russia with extremely dangerous potentials should Russia decide to do something foolish.

All the "boomers" that were left in the Navy were put to sea on an emergency basis and headed into areas where the Soviet Navy with its rusted out attack submarines could not touch them. The air forces of both countries began to arm their aircraft fully, to keep them fueled and ready to fly, and on some of them like the B-2 Stealth Bombers nuclear weapons were loaded. The B-2's began to fly training sorties out of Diego Garcia that lasted many hours. The B-2's crossed over much of Africa without entering into the air space of any unfriendly country. They carried bombs so destructive that their explosive results could not be adequately described.

China, seeing all these military preparations and worrying some of the missiles from the U.S. or Russia, or both, might be targeted in China, put its armed forces, including its nuclear missile units, on high alert as well. North Korea, as bellicose as ever, mouthed the usual phrases of being able to attack U.S. cities with its ICBMs. China was completely at sea over the reasons the U.S. and Russia were going "nuclear" all of a sudden. Yes, there had been an outbreak of Ebola in Crimea but it could have come about in a hundred different ways the Chinese thought. They were not prepared, as were the Russians, to toss the blame for the ebola occurrence squarely onto the shoulders of the U.S. The premier kept asking his political advisors, "How did this happen?" None of them seemed to have an answer.

But this is a little ahead of where it should be I guess. I was, when all this began, a member of the State Department. My name is William De Young. I was at one time an employee of an Undersecretary of State. What does that mean? Nothing really. It didn't give me information that others didn't have. It didn't tell me anything about Kalil or Falik. I guess I was a bit of a greenhorn as well. My graduation from Thomas Jefferson had taken place only about a year prior to the world melting down. I am thirty five years old. I had been working for Secretary of State Elizabeth Warren since she ascended to the position from her status as a Senator from the State of Massachusetts.

I can tell you we were scrambling around like crazy to try and find out who the hell had let off a weapon that included the Ebola virus as part of its destructive material. It still amazes me anyone, a human being, would let loose ebola. Have you ever seen a person die of Ebola virus, or any form of hemorrhagic fever? It is devastating. It is nasty looking. It is a mess. There is blood everywhere. Thankfully the victims were isolated quickly; well quickly being a word of art here because it took several days for recognition of the type of virus to occur. Then the victims were quickly isolated, proper protective clothing and breathing apparatus were used by the doctors and the spread of the disease was seemingly controlled to the point no new cases were being seen. But all through the time of the outbreak stuff was floating across all our desks in State like crazy. The one reaction I had to all this perhaps some did not was I began to think it was really possible for a nuclear exchange to occur between the United States and Russia.

When someone in the world gets a little crazy the rest of the world tends to react and most often their reaction is negative. Saudi Arabia, for example, threatened to turn off the oil spigot if there were another outbreak of this kind caused by the U.S. Caused by the U.S.? How the hell did they come to their conclusion? I personally spoke with a man whose job it was to operate the pipelines from the refineries to the shipping docks. He fairly screamed at me we in the U.S. were trying to kill off the world population of Muslims by the use of viral bombs. I said in return, "Sir, if I could confess to you to it was true and if it would be the truth, I would do so. But it is not the truth. The truth is the Russians don't know or understand where the viral attack came from and neither do we. Because the area is so tightly cordoned off in order to avoid new outbreaks we cannot even get in there to search for the weapon used to deliver the virus. But please, sir, we in the U.S. did not do this."

Letters went to every Prince, every Emir holding a position in the governments of Saudi Arabia, Qatar, Yemen; you name the person, we communicated with them. We constantly tried to reinforce the idea that we had nothing to do with the Ebola outbreak. It seemed as though we were speaking in tongues or to deaf people. No one believed us. The wrangle over Crimea and Ukraine going on since 2014 made us appear to be the likely culprit in the Ebola attack.

Kalil, seeing the responses of the Saudis and other oil rich Arab countries merely smiled to himself. He sent messages to his group of black shirted members of the ISIS forces. At least he sent letters to those whose lives had not ended in the bombing of their caravan. The letters told his brethren a new day was coming, to be prepared and ready to attack, attack, attack. Kalil's plans were diabolical indeed. His Sword of Fallujah organized fifteen truck bombs which would be sent into the domains of Maliki and the Shia in Baghdad and Muqtadr Al Sadr and his Shia militias at the same time. Kalil's spies had done their work well. The truck bombs were meant to trigger additional explosions from war materials hidden by the Shia in various places. The effect, if achieved, would be disastrous for the Shia militias and would make it possible for the Sunni to triumph with "little opposition."

Then slowly things eased up a little as the Ebola virus ran its course in the sick and isolated area in which it was now located. Then, one strange and horrible day, the world went to hell in a hurry. At about two o'clock in the afternoon Washington time a nuclear explosion occurred in Donetsk, sometimes called the capital of the eastern Ukraine. It devastated the entire city, killing tens of thousands instantly, destroying age old buildings as well as those newly constructed.

The government was not in session at the time, but all its representatives and officials lived within a ten mile radius of the capital building. They were killed, all of them. The power of the bomb was not huge by comparison to what would follow but it leveled an area of approximately thirty miles in every direction in which a mountain didn't slow the progress of the blast.

All totaled well over a million Ukrainian people were killed or injured in the blast. And in the blast and fire effects of the bomb many thousands of ethnic Russians and disguised Russian soldiers died as well. The troops had been surreptitiously taking part in the separatist efforts of the ethnic Russians in the Donetsk area. There were well over ten thousand Russian troops involved. Most of the troops were killed.

The "bloom" of the nuclear explosion was seen on every satellite within range. Some satellites had been placed in orbit by the Russians. Some had been placed there by the Chinese, the Japanese, the French and NATO via the French Ariadne series of launch vehicles and of course many had been placed there by the U.S. Some went dark within seconds after the explosion as a result of their components not being protected from the possibility of an EMP (Electro Magnetic Pulse) effect. Most of those were older and most belonged to the Soviets or the French and NATO.

The French, the British, the Germans, the Italians (nobody really expected them to fight if it came down to it), the Polish, among many other countries, were left pretty much in the dark as to what was going on between Russia and the U.S. But knowing the Americans were on high alert the French and British nuclear forces, as well as those of Israel, India and Pakistan were all alerted as precautionary measures.

Instantly the U.S. forces went to Defcon 3, nuclear attack alert and status for response by every means possible if someone might have the temerity to launch on the U.S. One country did, that being North Korea. None of the nuclear forces of the U.S. were launched initially since the Korean threat was so remote. No one could believe the Chinese would arm the Koreans with missiles which could reach the U.S. The response, if any were to occur from the United States, could be managed quite well without those assets.

A missile frigate sitting off the coast of Japan in the South China Sea saw the North Korean launch right away and launched an anti-missile in return. The Korean missile was destroyed at about 80,000 feet above the earth in a massive explosion that triggered the non-nuclear explosives on board the Korean bird. The Chinese radar systems had seen the launch, saw the second missile coming from the frigate which they routinely shadowed and saw the explosion of the two coming together.

A Chinese battery commander who was a nervous type anyway and who secretly admired the dictator of North Korea, ordered his anti-ship battery to fire at the frigate. At first his battery men looked at each other. They all knew this would constitute an act of war against the United States. But they were soldiers after all and they obeyed their orders. Three Chinese missiles of the same type as the French Exocets of earlier years now called the Kong Di 88 were launched by this battery. The radar units "painting" U.S.S. Glenn remained on, as did the television cameras on these missiles. The frigate responded instantly with newer HARM type missiles which would attack the radar but would cluster bomb the entire area as well.

The frigate, named the U.S.S. John Glenn, saw the launches from the mainland, knew they were being "painted" and fired up by radar and heat seeking missiles also using television capability. The frigate had defenses designed just for the purpose of bringing down the kind of missiles the Chinese fired. All three were splashed before reaching the frigate by missile or gunfire. The Chinese battery had to leave their radar on in order to guide their missiles and the battery was destroyed completely with substantial loss of life when the officer who had ordered the Frigate be fired upon failed to recognize that his facility was about to be attacked.

The Chinese Army saw this activity and ordered the Air Force to respond. The Air Force launched a dozen of its older Su-30 planes with missiles designed to attack ships as well as those used for attacking aircraft. In addition the Jengdu 10's (comparable in capabilities to the

U.S. F-16 and F-15E Strike Eagle aircraft) available near the area in which these events were unfolding were prepared to fight and then launched. There were more than twenty of those fine aircraft that flew sorties toward the U.S.S. Glenn.

The Chinese planes had not cleared their own borders when a flight of eight F-15 Strike Eagles whose systems had been highly upgraded by the Formosans were sent to investigate from Taipei, Formosa. An additional flight of eight F-15 E's with their systems upgraded by the Formosan's as well were launched from Tainan, Formosa. The Chinese Jengdus did not see these planes right away and the SU-30's of the Chinese never did see them. The first eight Formosan Air Force planes were "painted with radar" by the Chinese Air Force planes from over fifty miles away and the Chinese planes fired missiles at the Formosan planes who in turn fired missiles at the Chinese aircraft. An International "Cluster Fuck" was well under way. The Formosan aircraft from Tainan also fired missiles at both the SU-30's and the Jengdu 10's.

U.S. Air bases in Japan and Korea, hearing of the launch on the U.S. by the North Koreans, seeing the response of the Chinese to the DPRK missile being splashed, began to load their planes for war. The North Koreans fired another ICBM. The second was hit by an anti-missile missile fired again from the "Glenn." Several of the Chinese jets from the mainland got within range to launch their ship killing missiles. All totaled the Chinese launched at least ten ship killing missiles at the "Glenn." All of them but one were shot down. The one that was not killed by the ship sank the "Glenn." There were survivors but not many. The survivors would be picked up by Formosan boats. The Chinese aircraft which fired on the Glenn were all shot down by either U.S. or Formosan aircraft. In all the Chinese lost all of the SU-30 aircraft they launched toward the Glenn and half the Jengdu 10 aircraft.

Mostly the losses of the Chinese were due to the Formosans being in constant awareness and firing early on the Chinese aircraft. The North Koreans, undaunted, prepared, watched by a satellite, a third launch. They launched just before the end of the first fateful day of the international cluster fuck. Another missile frigate, stationed just north of the Island of Okinawa shot at that third North Korean ICBM. The hit on the Korean missile was enough to cause the payload to crash into the Pacific Ocean about 500 miles from Midway Island where it detonated one of its several nuclear warheads.

In the dark of night, just after dark in fact, four F-117 Stealth Fighters killed the launch facilities of the North Koreans without the loss of a plane. The launch pads of the Koreans would take weeks or months to reconstruct. The support facilities including the underground bunkers that housed the North Korean computer systems necessary to the launch of ICBMs were all destroyed as well. Those would take years to rebuild. The death of the computer center essentially ended the intermediate and short range missile threat to Seoul and South Korea in general except from shorter range missiles carried on mobile launchers. But the North Koreans had never acquired such sophistication with their nuclear arsenal they could miniaturize sufficiently to mount nuclear warheads on short range missiles.

The few ships of the Formosan navy that were in the rough area of the Glenn picked up the few survivors. The few planes lost by the U.S., Japan or Formosa also had their survivors picked up. While the missile launch facilities of the North Koreans were virtually eliminated their army and air forces were not. Immediately after the first launch all U.S. forces in Korea went on alert, as did all South Korean forces. Total call up occurred of all able bodied South Korean veterans who were still capable of fighting. The situation there was out of hand. The situation with the Chinese began to calm when the U.S. began to pull its citizens out of the country. The loss of business activity was instant and the Chinese, ever mindful of economics, apologized for the "inadvertent actions" of a rogue officer who had been executed for his traitorous launch of planes and missiles at the U.S. ship.

The Chinese, ever masters of the apology, offered reparations for the sinking of the Glenn and for the families of the lost seamen. This calmed the situation in respect to China but not as to Korea. China did say as long as there was no invasion of North Korea which might threaten its borders China would stay out of any fracas between the North and South Koreans.

The momentary detente with the Chinese allowed the U.S. to assist the South Korean Air Force against the North Koreans. Virtually all hard protective revetments that the North Koreans had created to protect their Air Forces were destroyed in one night. All their runways were so badly cratered, as were the taxi ways along side their air fields, that the North Korean air forces were eliminated in one night. What few North Korean aircraft that did escape the bombing went into China to be grounded.

That left the A-10's of the U.S. and the South Koreans to strike under the cover of F-16s and F-15 Strike Eagles of the South Koreans and the F-35s of the U.S. along with the FA-18 naval aircraft of the U.S., at the columns of troops, tanks, etc. being marshaled by the North Koreans for an attack on the South. The North Korean army, a million plus in numbers at the beginning of that day, lost at least a third of their troops within thirty-six hours. They also lost almost all their transport systems, a large part of their tank brigades, and almost all of their helicopters and transport aircraft carrying airborne troops. All in all the vaunted members of the North Korean Army and other forces were badly treated by the South Koreans and the U.S. forces the first couple of days of the brief war in which they engaged. The South Koreans maintained an open channel with the Chinese to make sure that the Chinese understood there would be no northward thrust of South Korean forces if the North Koreans stood down. It was over the next day.

The uneasy truce between North Korea and South Korea, with the U.S. as participants along the lines of demarcation, resumed. But the Chinese influence on the North Koreans became of extreme importance to the continuation of the regime. China allowed the U.N. to bring in nuclear scientists. The U.N. representatives stripped the North Koreans of any further ability by missile or otherwise, to deliver a nuclear weapon in addition to destroying all their existing weapons, destroying all records of how to assemble or create a nuclear weapon. One thing good came out of the short war. The short war with North Korea also gave the Russians pause for consideration of their desire to confront the American beast. But the events of Ukraine caused caution to be thrown in the wind.

The tensions between Washington and Moscow had escalated all through the several days of the Korean fiasco. Nastiness was the hallmark of the communication between President Clinton and Premier Putin. He considered her a person of lesser import in part because she was a woman. His attitude made the likelihood of real communication impossible from the outset. The world conflicts and troubles in the Middle East made him even more bellicose and unreasonable. She could not "give" much or she would be seen as weak not only by Putin but by her own military. In the circumstance she must maintain control of the military. The mistakes of the Chinese and Russians already had shown her that necessity.

In spite of the recommendations of her military adviser's advice, President Clinton backed off the military alert status to Defcon 2. That meant stand down of some weapons but readiness maintained for immediate launch of those weapons if necessary. The Russians appeared to be relaxing their nuclear forces as well and the world heaved a huge sigh of relief as a moment of sanity seemed to form in both countries. Sanity has a way of giving in to misunderstanding though. So does insanity. All over the Mediterranean Sea American ships patrolled at the ready. The same was true of the Indian Ocean where in addition to U.S. ships there were ships of the nation of India as well.

Pakistan and India had co-existed with armed nuclear weapons aimed at each other for over 25 years. And the fingers of their leaders had been very close to the "buttons" during the crisis over the terrorist activities in Mumbai. The threat of Pakistan was now enhanced by the potential of a Shia caliphate running from Iran through Iraq into Syria and Lebanon. The possibility also existed of even more area to be garnered by the Shia in the other "stans" of the former Soviet Union and of course in Afghanistan. Pakistan, seeing the threat of a loss by the Shia as a great possibility before the nuclear detonation in Ukraine, was more frightened after the nuclear blast occurred. The Pakistanis immediately thought the Sunni had done the deed. They suggested it to the Russians. The Russians laughed at them and said it could not have happened as the Pakistanis suspected.

We requested the Chinese to bring their "boomers" to the surface so we could see them. Though they were loathe to do so they complied with our request. The former Soviet fleet of "boomers" and other submarines aside from their attack subs had long since either been sold to China, India, Iran or North Korea. The satellite and drone system essentially watching all of North Korea knew exactly where their subs were located.

The U.S. announced to China and North Korea that if the North Korean submarines made one belligerent move their entire sub fleet would be sunk. One general in North Korea thought the statement was hyperbolae and caused the launch of a cruise missile which narrowly missed the main government buildings of Seoul. The U.S. Navy sank a total of fifteen subs that day. The North Koreans had one left in dry dock and it was destroyed by a stealth attack from a Navy F-35 stealth fighter aircraft.

The Russians threatened nuclear war if any further attacks occurred on North Korea. The Pakistani government, allied with Russia since 2018, announced its support for the Russians. India went to high alert. Israel went to high alert when Iran announced its support for the Russian statements against the U.S. A Pakistani pilot thought he saw a drone over the northern part of the country and fired several missiles at what he thought was a drone. He missed.

The drone pilot was good and the drone was a stealth version just put into service which was armed with anti-aircraft missiles as well as air to ground ordnance. The drone pilot didn't miss. There were Indian aircraft in the area. The Pakistanis had just received very sophisticated radar systems from Russia and were not terribly good at using those systems yet. They saw the Indian aircraft, saw one of their own being destroyed and started firing ground to air missiles at the Indian aircraft.

The nearest of the three Indian aircraft carriers armed its planes and sent all its fighters toward the area of conflict along with AWACS aircraft in support. MIG 35 aircraft from Goa, in India, also headed toward the area of conflict. The AWACS reported "seeing" what appeared to be a missile silo opening. It was, but for a ground to air missile attacking the flight of Indian SU-30 and MIG-35 aircraft. The air burst of the missile was larger than usual to the pilots of the Indian aircraft and it threw an instant mushroom characteristic of a nuclear explosion. The AWACS operators were not familiar with nuclear explosions and did not take the time to use their instruments to explore the type of chemicals in the explosion. They reported a nuclear blast. India opened its silos. Pakistan opened its silos.

My boss was on the phone on one side of her head to New Delhi, on the other side of her head to Islamabad. She kept saying, "Gentlemen, please, calm down, let's talk for a few minutes. What can a few minutes of your time mean to all your people? The course you are headed down could potentially destroy both your countries." Then she would sit and listen for a moment and then again she would begin, "Gentlemen, gentlemen, please, talk with me for a moment. Talk with me, not each other just for a moment." Then she would listen again and then she would start all over again. This went on and on and on for what seemed like an interminable time. And then wonderfully we got word from satellite photography over India and Pakistan the silo doors had closed. Thank God, I kept thinking. What in the hell are they trying to accomplish? What in the hell is Russia doing here? Are they the instigators of all this?

The next satellite image we saw was a missile launch from Iran, and then a second launch from Iraq. Where in the hell did they get any missiles? The missiles came from the western part of Iraq, long under the control of the Sunni insurgents, the ISIS groups. Then a third launch came from Northern Lebanon. The Iron Dome system installed years earlier by Israel shot down the Lebanese launch practically before it was off the ground. The launch from Iraq was handled by a missile frigate in the Sixth Fleet at relatively low altitude. There was a secondary explosion of the Iranian missile that was spectacular to see on the satellite photos.

The third launch, or the first in the series came from Iran. It could only be ballistic. A number of Patriot batteries fired at it while it was incoming over first Iraq and then part of Jordan. Jordan even fired at it not knowing if it was meant for Jordan or Israel. The Iron Dome system in Israel flooded the sky with shots at the Iranian missile as it fired its own ballistic missile at Teheran.

It was clear when the Iranian missile was finally hit that it had a huge warhead on board or maybe nuclear. Crews were sent to the areas of the debris field that was created from the secondary explosions on the Iranian missile. They found radioactive material all over the debris field just as the Israeli missile slammed into the government buildings of the Teheran government.

Israel launched its entire Air Force at that moment in a defensive maneuver, and many of its planes were armed with air to ground missiles. And many of those missiles contained nuclear warheads. The planes that held the nukes stayed at sea, well away from the coastal defenses of the Lebanese Hezbollah militias and the elements of the Syrian military which still occupied parts of Lebanon. The Syrians, thinking they could take advantage of the situation, attacked the Golan Heights installations of the Israelis. As usual the Israelis used air power and better tanks than the Syrians possessed to beat back those attacks, take the offensive themselves and drive the Syrian forces back to Damascus.

While the Syrians were attacking Northern Israel the Sunnis in Iraq decided to do the same thing. They tried to go through Jordan. Jordan's forces held long enough to ask the U.S. Fleet for needed air power to stop the attack. It was stopped and pushed back into Iraq with the Sunnis suffering yet another Highway of Death. The Iranians used the attack of the Sunnis to bring most of their Republican Guard units into Iraq. They numbered over one hundred thousand. When the Sunnis limped back toward Tikrit the Shia Iranian forces attacked with heavy artillery, tanks and air power and decimated the Sunni forces. Kalil's ploys were at an end and the best he and his cronies could do was escape into Syria. The Iranians, allied with the Shia of Iraq.

The Syrians welcomed their fellow Sunni fighters and stopped the attacks of the Iranian forces at the Syrian border roughly. While all this was going on a missile weapons platform was reconstructed in Israel that had Iran's markings all over it. And two of the three warheads that had not exploded out of the seven on the platform, were found to be nuclear. Israel started diplomatic measures against Iran right away. It also launched an air raid that leveled the entire complex from which the Iranian missiles had been launched at Israel. Seeing all this happening I kept thinking to myself sooner or later sane and calmer heads are going to prevail. But I was so very wrong.

My folks lived in Omaha for a long time. It is the nerve center of the Strategic Air Command, or the missile and bomber command of the U.S. Air Force. I don't know why but I told them to get out of Omaha the day of the first explosion in Donetsk. They took me at my word. They were both retired and had developed a piece of property in the mountains near Missoula, Montana. They went to Montana.

The day of the missile attack on Israel I sent my wife and children to Butte, Montana where they were picked up by my folks after a three part flight out of Philadelphia. I was nearly too late. But mom and dad, and my kids and my wife, were safe in the mountains of Montana. Then I decided it was time for a vacation myself, and I took off by car from Washington, D.C. Gas prices steadily went higher every day. It was the same for food. Had I waited one more day, I would never have made it through Nebraska.

The Iranians in Iraq began to rain down missiles containing regular high explosive warheads on Israel as soon as they had control of virtually the entire country of Iraq. I sent my wife and kids away. Russia began to put long diatribes on television against the United States and continued to blame the U.S. for the Ebola outbreak and the explosion of a nuclear weapon in Donetsk. They promised retaliation. They delivered one piece of retaliation by sinking two missile cruisers and damaging a nuclear aircraft carrier in the Mediterranean Sea.

The attack came from at least two dozen air fired SSN-22-Sunburn missiles. The frigates and cruisers were able, along with the aircraft carrier to shoot down all but three with various defensive systems. The three missiles hit the two cruisers. One other missile was destroyed by a defensive gun so close to the carrier that its detonation damaged the superstructure of the carrier. There was a predictable outcry from around the U.S. and a lot of very loud and courageous talk from white haired old men. They would not fight if war started. They had never fought but would be perfectly willing to send some other person's child off to war. War was already started according to them. My guess is their sons and daughters, for the most part, would never know anything about war.

The military power structure was openly critical of President Clinton when she did not respond to this attack within 24 hours with at least as severe a bombing of Russian assets. Much of those 24 hours she was on the phone with Putin. Secretary of State Warren was everywhere on television, pleading for sanity and willingness to look past this affront. But none of the speeches made any difference.

The aircraft carrier was still launching planes even though damaged. The frigates and destroyers protecting the carrier from subs and aerial attacks still had cruise missiles at their disposal as well as defensive missiles. They used them in immediate response to the Russian attack without reference to the attempts at diplomacy. Their attack was on the Russian fleet in the Black Sea, most of which was docked at Sevastopol. The Navy attack was devastatingly effective. Nearly the entire Russian fleet of ships which had sailed on top of the water were sunk in one blow. The tunnels in Sevastopol housing the remaining Russian submarine fleet were also closed by this attack from the Sixth Fleet ships. Aerial warfare between the American carrier based planes and Russian land based planes began at the same time the fleet responded to the Russian missile attack. Everything diplomatic went awry. Putin slammed the phone in the ear of the president and screamed in Russian at her she would not live to regret this attack on his country. The rest of the response was predictable as well and triggered nuclear war all over the planet. Russia launched first thinking it would be able to destroy the few remaining Minutemen missiles the U.S. had in silos in Montana and the Dakotas. Russia's initial strike was at those silos as well as at Thunder Mountain and Omaha along with Washington, D.C. The anti-missile system the U.S. had begun to develop under President Reagan and continued to perfect from then on worked very well. One Russian missile was launched at Washington, D.C. It failed to come close to the United States after being partially destroyed by an anti-missile strike. But it was not the only missile sent toward D.C.

The numbers of ICBMs that the Russians launched were an extreme surprise to the military leaders of the U.S. Several Russian missiles struck Omaha despite heavy anti-missile successes. Several Russian missiles struck the areas of the silos in Montana and the Dakotas but were unsuccessful in destroying the Minuteman sites which had answered with a launch less than ten minutes after the first missile came off Russian soil. Satellite observation of the Russian launch made the defense of the U.S. much more effective. The Russians did not launch EMP strikes at satellites as they were afraid of killing their own eyes in the sky as well as those of the U.S.

Pakistan, seeing this occurring on its satellites, launched against New Delhi and other targets in India. India launched against Pakistan. Russia launched more missiles southward toward Israel. Israel struck back. Iran tried to launch again but failed when stealth bombers from Israel destroyed its launch facilities. Israel launched or sent low flying aircraft carrying nuclear weapons against Iran, Syria, Iraq and Lebanon.

All over the Mediterranean standard weaponry flew in every direction. Russia hit Germany, France and England as well as the United States. France and England struck back seeing the launches against their countries. Millions upon millions of tonnage of explosive power was unleashed all over the world in what seemed to many as the start of Armageddon. But it was not the end. Instead, it was the beginning.

BOOK I
THE TREK,
WAR BEGINS AT HOME

In war, attack is the secret of defense;
defense is the planning of an attack.
Great results can be achieved with small forces.
Sun Tzu, The Art of War

Chapter 1

Heading West

It was not I was foretelling any of the events that occurred, the god-awful devastation that took place and caused me to leave Washington. It's just I wanted to take off and see my folks, my kids and my wife again before... before... oh hell it was so evident that it was coming to us all in D.C. I got out when I could. My kids and my wife and my parents all were in a safe place because I had the sense to tell them to get out while the getting was good. Many of us did. Some, the unlucky ones, didn't or didn't get out themselves. It was the second round of missiles, bombers, submarine launched destruction which destroyed our whole damn world. By then I was with my family.

As I crossed the Mississippi River into Nebraska and cruised west of Omaha to near the border of Nebraska, Colorado and Wyoming I saw the blooms of the missiles hitting Omaha. I was lucky. I had been able to fill up with gas twice after seeing the hits. I knew what they were but there was still electric power to the towns where I stopped in Wyoming. And people apparently either were not aware yet of the blasts in Omaha or didn't know what to do about them yet. I was seeing a lot of uniforms by then, a lot of camouflage, a lot of army equipment. I took the southern route across Wyoming on I-80 because I thought maybe Montana and the Dakotas might have gotten hit the same time as Omaha. It turned out to be a good deduction I would find out later.

My assumption from seeing the uniforms was that the military units of the National Guard and Reserve units had been called up and were mobilizing to protect the people from themselves. It seemed evident martial law was on the way. I hoped to make it past Idaho Falls before running into roadblocks. Again I was lucky. About half way out of Idaho Falls and Dillon, Montana, where again I had gotten gas and a little food, as I headed toward Missoula on I-15 I got stopped in a long line of cars and trucks.

The wait was long. Almost all the cars that were in front of me, or so it seemed to me, turned around and headed back toward the south right away after coming to the actual roadblock. When I was about three cars away I could see there was a roadside rest stop next to the highway into which a few cars were being diverted before being allowed to proceed north. The rest of the cars were being told to turn around. I was still in Idaho but just barely.

The roadblock was being operated jointly by the Idaho State Police and the army as far as I could tell. I only saw regular patrol officers of the Idaho State Police but there were a couple of U.S Army trucks there with machine guns mounted on them as well as searchlights. The machine guns had cartridge belts fed into them I could see from the roadblock. When I was two cars from the stop a policeman came by my car and said to me "Where are you headed?"

I replied "Missoula."

He said, "Pull into the roadside rest when you get to the entrance. You will be given instructions and information there." I followed his directions when I got into the rest stop area, where there were not a lot of cars, and where most of the people were walking toward one of the buildings in the center. It looked like a set of bathrooms but it had a kiosk in the center with maps and information boards. The information boards were in between two buildings which turned out to be the restrooms. As I stopped at the direction of another patrol officer he pointed me into a parking slot and walked to my car as I got out and stood up. He said to me "Assume the position."

I had no idea what he meant. I made a gesture with my hands meaning what? He said "Turn around, put your hands on top of the car, lean forward and back up with your feet until you can feel tension in the back of your legs." I followed his instructions very carefully. He had a hand on a pistol the entire time. When I was in position he searched me, cuffed me and stood me beside my car. He took my keys, turned the engine off for a moment, searched the interior of my car, got out and searched the trunk after opening it, then came back to me and un-handcuffed me.

As he took the cuffs off me I asked "What's going on? I don't mean to be a smart ass, but why all this?"

"We have had some militia boys try to come through here carrying a lot of weapons," he said, "so we are being a little careful. Some of them thought they would establish a different authority than the government. So we are making sure no one else gets a chance to try anything, at least not in this area. Okay, go to the center of the buildings and listen to what they are saying there. What is your final destination?"

"Just on the other side of Missoula in the area of Frenchtown."

"Yeah. I know that area pretty well. I have done some deer hunting up there. Okay. You seem to have enough gas to get there easily. But you might get some here from the Rangers if you need it. You won't find any more gas available as you head up there. You will be allowed to go to Missoula, but you are likely to be stopped by roving patrols. On the other side of Missoula somewhere up by Kellog, Idaho there will be another roadblock you will have to go through if you go that far. You should not try to g there. We will be sending the information on your car to that roadblock and if you get there, after what you have told me here you will be turned around. Go ahead now and listen to the instructions they are giving up there."

As I walked to the area between the bathrooms I saw a man and a woman talking quietly with a group of twenty or thirty others. They had not started the group session yet. As I stepped up behind the rest they began. The man said "Hi folks. My name is Ray Wheaton. My friend here is Mona James. We both work for the State of Idaho as park rangers. We have been asked to tell you what is going on as it has been given to us by the patrol and the army." The woman just waved a little kind of friendly hello gesture and said nothing.

Ray continued saying "It is true that the United States has been attacked by Russia. It is also true many other countries are involved in an exchange of nuclear weapons and regular war-like actions. In fact Montana was hit in several places to the east and north of Butte. Likewise a lot of places in North and South Dakota have been hit as well. Had you told the officer at the roadblock that you were headed east or toward Yellowstone, or toward the Dakotas, you would have been told to go home and turned around. Since you are headed west and no strikes have come to the west coast yet we are going to let you go on as far as you can. There are some problems you will have to be aware of though."

There was some milling around, some coughing, some gasps during the first part of Ray's comments. I was not surprised by his announcement about the nuclear strikes. I had seen the blooms above Omaha. But I had been lucky enough to have enough distance between Omaha and my car so the EMP results of the blasts did not kill my car. I was not surprised to know that eastern Montana and the Dakotas had been hit as well. After all the few Minuteman Missiles we had left had been in hardened silos in those places.

Ray continued. He said, "You folks that are headed toward Missoula will be directed immediately onto the appropriate road as you leave Dillon, Montana. You will be able to stay on I-15 that far. But please do not try and go off the highway between here and there. Militias have taken control of a number of communities in Idaho and Montana. We think Dillon might be one of those. We are not even sure our normal law enforcement or even our laws still exist in some places in Idaho and Montana. So as you drive north and especially after you begin to go through the mountains into Missoula be very careful. If you see a car stopped do not, I repeat, do not stop to see if you can help unless it is a patrol car and only then if you can see two officers. All our police cruisers will travel with two officers from now on, everywhere in Montana, Idaho, everywhere on the west coast and eastward as far as there is an eastward. And we just don't know about that other than Omaha. It is gone."

Someone in the crowd asked, "What do you mean Omaha is gone?"

"Exactly what I said. Omaha does not exist any longer. Up to three and maybe more missile strikes hit the area with high yield weapons. It has been obliterated. Okay. If any of you need gasoline we are authorized to let you fill your tanks from our stores here. Once the gas is gone though you will not find any gasoline available anywhere again. Did you understand what I just said?"

Everyone nodded and shuffled off toward their cars. Some of them had children along with them. Some of the children and the women were crying. I heard one of them say to her husband, "Oh God, my sister, her family, oh God, Gene, they must all be gone." She burst out in sobs then. One of the men walked over to the officer who had searched me and said, "I had a pistol in my car that you took from me. Can I have it back? We might need it for our protection."

"No. We are trying to disarm everyone with guns. We don't want any more weapons to fall into the hands of the militias than they already have. If you are stopped by a militia group and you try to fight them you will be killed along with everyone in your family except maybe your oldest daughter. If you have nothing they need, no guns or ammunition perhaps they will not bother you. No one will be allowed to have guns once we get them all collected unless there is a necessity for an armed force to be gathered together from the survivors amongst you."

Though my gas tank was mostly full I calculated if I ran all the way to Missoula I would be short about five gallons to get into the mountains just east of there where my family was located. So I got into line and filled up. The Rangers walked up and down the line and gave each of us a couple of bottles of water and a couple of sacks of stuff like Cheetos.

They told us if we left the freeway at any point before Missoula they did not know if it was safe. We might not find food or water under any circumstance, they said. They also said by the time we got to Missoula they couldn't be sure of what we would find there. The one thing that frightened me a lot which they told us as we were leaving was, as it was put to us by Ray, "Don't be on the road after dark in any area where there are no towns or where you do not see roadblocks like this one. If you are, find what appears to be a safe place to hide you and your car, go to sleep if you can and stay there until after dawn. Under any circumstance don't come back here after dark. We will not be here. This area is infested with militiamen or those who would take whatever you have of value. They rule the night. We leave and go into a compound which is heavily fortified near here. So don't come back here."

It was only a couple of hours to Missoula though and it seemed to me there was still plenty of daylight left so I thought it should be all right. In a little while I was back on the freeway headed north. In less than an hour I made the turnoff onto I-90 to the mountains. There were patrol vehicles and military both blocking the road east to Butte. No one was allowed to go toward Butte. There were not a lot of cars on the road for sure. In my first hour of driving I passed one car and had two others pass me.

There were no trucks at all. But I guess that should be expected. Many of the trucks that used to be (used to be, oh my God what a thought) on the highway were gasoline trucks headed to fill the tanks of local fuel outlets. Many others were food trucks of one kind or another filled with packaged foods.

Between Butte and Missoula there are a series of small mountain passes. I don't remember the heights you get up to, maybe as high as four or five thousand feet. But the road is good, freeway for the most part and four lane where it is not freeway. It's easy driving, but one has to pay attention or it would be easy to be going too fast and maybe slide off the road. I slowed a little for one car which had done just that.

It was kind of teetering on the edge of the dirt berm next to the high-way. I didn't see anyone in the car and there were no highway patrol cars around so I took the Rangers at their word and kept on going.

As I passed by I saw a guy come out of the woods with a rifle in his hand and a woman being dragged by the hair behind him. I couldn't tell if she was dead or alive. And there was nothing I could do to help her. God. Apparently it had started already. What did the guy expect to get from the woman? What would he do with her afterward? Why? Had our legalistic society broken down so much in such a short period of time?

I began to think then about how I could arm myself. In the trunk of the car, under the spare tire where the patrol officer who searched my car did not look, there was a K-Bar folding knife I used for carving things. It had a four or five inch blade on it. I supposed if push came to shove and I had to use a knife to defend myself it would be effective. But if someone came at me with a gun what would I do? There would be nothing I could do. God knows with a quarter million guns or more floating around in our society there were plenty of people who had them.

As the day began to wane I began to worry about getting to French-town before dark. What about Frenchtown itself? I had to go through there to get to the mountain where my folks had their place. It was a typical small town with its own city council, its own sanitation de-partment, its own police department. It was also a highly patriotic and demonstrative town when it came to our country. Bunting was always hung, the year round. Flags flew the year round, and people were en-gaged in a constant debate over politics. It also seemed to be true most of the people there espoused the conservative viewpoint. Would there be a militia group there?

There was a small college campus in Frenchtown. It was why the town existed at all. It was how my dad got acquainted with the area. He visited there one year as a political science professor. After being there for about six months he bought a parcel of land in the forest, built a smallish home on the land and would go back during the months it was not covered by snow to do work on it. Or at least my folks would tell me about his work on the house when I called them. I had only been there once before. It was not easy to find. It was not on a road or beaten track of any kind.

It was what my dad wanted, a place he could go to which was not easy to find and where he could be free from other people around him. Why he wanted solitude I could not get out of him. When I would ask my mother about the topic she would say "Oh, you know it's just your father." There would have to be some additional commentary about the topic when I arrived at his place.

And then the second anomaly of the day happened when a pick-up truck pulled out of a side road and began to follow me. I could see there were a couple of guys in the bed of the pick-up with rifles in their hands. The speed limit in the area was fifty-five because of the mountainous road, and some curvy up and down areas. I saw an exit ahead. As I drew closer to the exit I could see some other pick-up trucks parked near the stop sign at the bottom of a hill.

The exit didn't seem to go to any town. The truck pulled along side me and the guy in the right seat waved at me with a pistol and pointed toward the exit. It was getting close. As I came closer to the exit I began to slow as though I were going to go off the freeway. The truck stayed right with me for a time and then dropped behind me as we came abreast of the exit. I punched it and went as fast as the car would go to get the hell out of there.

I started hearing shots behind me. The pick-up had stopped and the guys with rifles were shooting at me. I thought they had missed, must be poor shooters, until one of their bullets impacted the rear window and shattered it. I kept going as fast as I could and soon I was out of their sight. I kept driving way too fast for the conditions for a long way. As I neared Missoula and could actually see the town nestled down into a beautiful valley, there were two state patrol cars parked by the road on my side. I slowed down and waited until I could see four officers. I stopped next to them and told them what had happened. They said thanks and they would let the army know. Let the army know? What the hell? I didn't argue with them for sure. I asked them "Are there any more patrol cars on the other side of Missoula?"

One of them who was wearing Sergeant's stripes said "Oh yeah, you must be that guy that's going to Frenchtown. Yes," he said, "there are a couple of other cars along the way up there. But they may be too far away from Frenchtown exit to do you any good if you have trouble before you get there. So be aware just like you were back there. By the way if you had pulled over those boys would have shot you just for the gasoline that remains in your car, however much it might be."

*The title of Recon Marine is my honor.
I shall never quit. I will overcome, adapt,
do what is necessary.*
From Force Recon Marine Credo

Chapter 2

Almost Home

With a great deal of relief and thanks to the patrolmen I went on into Missoula. I had drawn a sizable amount of cash out of my bank account in D.C. before I left there so in various places in the car I had stashed some cash. I stopped at a Micky "D"s that appeared to be open just off the freeway. It was, and I was able to buy the most highly priced double cheeseburgers I had ever paid for, at twenty dollars apiece with a coke that cost me five dollars. I guess everyone has to make it while they can. It looked to me like they were closing up. But at least I got to eat something besides Cheetos. It was the first "real" food I had eaten since well before Omaha.

I wolfed down the sandwiches and Coke as I drove further west toward Frenchtown. It was around ten miles out of town where I would turn off to go to Frenchtown. I made a road change I had forgotten just outside Missoula and at that point I became worried. Right after the road change there was a sign giving an exit number which said Frenchtown. I saw a small road going off the highway in front of me. There were no other cars traveling the road at all. I took the road.

Where would it go? Not far, for sure, because it ended at a home in the forest.

There were no signs of life at the home. No smoke was coming out of the fireplace chimney along one side of the house. No cars were there. There was nothing to indicate life. It turned out there was a reason for the lifelessness of the place.

I pulled around to the back of the house where my car could not be seen from the road. There were a lot of tire tracks back there. I couldn't make any sense of them. It looked like someone had done donuts in the dirt with a large vehicle, but again there were no signs of life. I went to the back door of the house and knocked. The screen door on the back of the house had been torn off and thrown aside off the small deck area leading to the back door. When I knocked on the door no one answered, but the door moved. It was open. I pushed it further open.

I puked over the side of the deck immediately. The residents of the house, at least two of them, were seated at the dining room table in the kitchen area. They had been cut repeatedly across the face and neck and upper body. Their clothing on the upper body was gone. The woman's breasts were nearly gone. The man was slashed so badly across his chest that you could not tell whether he had nipples left or not. Apparently after the torture inflicted on them the couple had been shot between the eyes one at a time. They had been dead for quite a while. They smelled pretty badly. There was a small shed like structure behind the house. I took them out there one by one and covered them with some blankets I found in the shed then went back into the house. I didn't think there would be much I could gain by being there but I thought maybe I could find out who the old couple were and report their deaths when I got to my dad's house.

There was very little left in the refrigerator. The door to the refrigerator had been standing open for some time so the food was all rotten. I threw it all into a trash bag and found a trash can outside into which I put the rotten mess. I didn't know what the hell else I should do so I just sat down and cried for a while. I made a decision. It was about two to three miles to Frenchtown from where I was, I thought. It seemed pretty much a certainty to me if I attempted to drive the distance someone was going to stop me and kill me. Obviously, based on where I was and what I had seen, all civil authority in Frenchtown had broken down. My next thought was I wondered how far out into the forest whoever had done this was ranging. I wondered if they had gotten to my dad's place yet.

My father is a retired teacher. He retired after a relatively short career as a college prof teaching political science. He is also a retired Marine Corps Lieutenant Colonel. He was first a Marine Lieutenant, commanding a Platoon, then a First Lieutenant commanding a platoon, then a Captain, commanding a company of Marines.

Then he became Recon. He made Major while commanding a company of Recon Marines and ended up as a Lt. Colonel in charge of a battalion of Recon Marines. He retired from teaching not because it was time he did but because he was tired of working. He and my mom were frugal all their lives. They had to be as a military couple. The result was they had a large savings and a fair amount of monthly income from his military days. He also had been able to retire from both the teaching profession and to draw Social Security for a period of years prior to the nuclear war with Russia.

My dad's name is Eugene de Young. My mother is named Irene. My wife's name is Carolyn Ruth. We call her Ruthie. My two boy's names are Gene and Billy. They should all be together at the "cabin." And if anyone tried to go there and mess with them as they had with this family a shit storm would have ensued. My father has guns, lots of them, some military weapons, and through the years he has gathered a lot of ammunition. He has always had a belief there might come a time when it would be necessary for him to use those weapons for the benefit of his family.

His "cabin" was built just for the reason the world might go on a total cluster fuck as it has! He built it in mind of nuclear war. He incorporated a lot of natural rock formations into the construction. He did almost all the work himself. He alone knew all the nuances of the defenses he built into the property. I was not so worried about whether they might all be okay but I was worried about how many might have gone to his place, what they might have found, what might have happened there.

But the mess I found at this place showed me I could not get to my dad's place by car. So now I had to figure out how I could walk there, whether I could defend myself if I had to, how to be able to defend myself, and how to avoid detection above all. It was only about two or three miles into Frenchtown, probably a mile through the town to the roads into the mountains and then maybe ten miles back to my dad's place.

It was maybe a total of fifteen miles distance from where I was located at the time. I had no doubt I could get there, could walk there, could even run part of it if I were put into the position of having to do so. But how to keep from being detected? Darkness would have to become my friend. It had been before and could be again.

My car had to be put completely out of sight in case we could come back to it later on. There had been a gas station next to the Micky "D"s in Missoula. They sold me 10 gallons for two hundred dollars. I had to try and preserve the gas in case we had the opportunity to head for the west coast. I knew no explosions had occurred west of Montana up to the time of my arrival in Frenchtown area anyway.

I scouted around the property and found there was a kind of natural area behind the shed where the car could be parked and it had a sort of recess in which the car could be concealed. I put the car into the recess, took some branches and obscured the tire tracks, scattered some pieces of tree limbs around and on the car to help it look more natural and went out to see how it looked. I could not see the car.

The hamburgers I ate in Missoula left me. I was hungry but didn't know if there was anything in the house which might be edible. I started searching around and found a package of pemmican in the master bedroom just under the side of the bed where the man must have slept. Apparently after the people who were there killed the occupants they didn't do much of a search. As I ate I decided to do a little more searching. Who knows what I might find, I thought.

I found, in a shoe box in the top of the closet, a .45 pistol. It looked old, the handle was a little slick, the clip was in it and there were rounds in the clip. It laid in the box next to a badge from San Diego Police Department. There were some extra rounds in the box and another clip there as well. I took the time to load some of the shells into the clip and while I was loading those rounds I found a kind of recess in the closet the killers had missed as well.

Inside the recess there was a safe. I left it alone. There was also some cash laying loose in the area. I took the cash. There was a shotgun that was not designed for hunting. It was loaded with a number of rounds and had a sleeve on the stock with more. There was also a box in the recess with more 12 gauge shells. I looked through the recess with the shotgun and found that there was one more thing in it. That was an

AR-15 rifle with a full clip as well as several other full clips laying loose next to the rifle. There was a Sam Browne in the closet recess as well with a holster that fit the .45 pistol. I put the Sam Browne on and it fit well enough not to bounce around much.

In the closet, boxed, there were some good hiking boots. I checked the size which happened to be exactly the same as mine. There was a good down coat which would come in handy for night walking. It was summer but the nights would still be cold. I went out to my car and got a thermal undershirt I had packed along with some thermal shorts and socks. There was a backpack in the car I took as well. I felt badly about the house and the stuff that I was taking but I supposed if the guy was going to have someone take his belongings he would probably prefer me to those who killed him. I loaded some fresh underwear and socks from my suitcase into the backpack along with a couple of extra shirts and went back into the house.

I went through the kitchen quickly and found very little there to eat. The killers had taken almost everything by way of canned goods. They missed a couple of cans of kipper snacks and a package of crackers. I figured the crackers and kippers could be one day's food. I put it into the pack. I found a little cold cereal left in one of the cabinets. I ate it. I found a door to a cellar which didn't seem to have been disturbed. It was one of those arrangements where a recessed wall ironing board came down out of it. The board was down like the woman had been ironing when the men came. The door handle to the cellar was hidden. I went down into the cellar after trying the wall switch. I was amazed to see there was still power to the house and then I realized I had heard a generator running outside somewhere.

I went downstairs and found a treasure trove of small canned goods that the killers had missed. I loaded as much of that as I could into my backpack and then loaded up a plastic bag set that I doubled up and tied it to my back pack. It was heavy and awkward and I had to adjust it to keep it from rubbing me in places as I walked. It was almost dark by then and I had no clue what I would do about walking except which direction I had to go. The last thing I found which was a godsend was a hat that had ear protection on it. There were some binoculars on a bench in the basement. I took them though I knew they would be useless except in the daylight hours, but I thought I might have some use for them at some point.

As I went upstairs I shut off the lights and started to walk into the kitchen just about the time another car pulled up in front of the house. It was a police car. I didn't dare let them find me. As I slipped out the back door and ran into the forest, I heard them knocking on the door and calling out the name Scotty. I grabbed the rifle and shotgun with all the other stuff on the way out. I made very little noise and they were making a lot. I don't think they heard me. It was already dark in the woods which I ran into. By the time I got there I saw a flashlight go on and head for the back of the house. Then I heard the other one in front say "You know if they are not here they must be in town. And if they are not in town then they are dead. You know what is going on out here. These damned militias are killing anyone they find alone now. And it's getting late and those bastards will be taking control of the roads soon. Let's get the hell out of here." The one with the flashlight stopped, turned slightly toward the rear of the house, then turned around and muttering to himself went back and got into the car. The two cops left in a hurry.

Though I knew it was time to get going myself I decided to make myself a bed in the cellar, leave the ironing board down as it had been, hope that no one found the door to the cellar and do some initial movement and scouting in the morning early. I didn't want to be trapped down there so I looked around carefully before bedding down and found another door which seemed to go outside. It appeared to be locked from the outside. I went around the house, found the door and unlocked it. Then I went down into the cellar and made myself a comfortable spot, ate a can of kipper snacks and some crackers and went to sleep. When I awakened it was still dark. Someone was moving around in the house. I heard them.

I slowly and carefully scattered my bed area and waited. The scuffling seemed to stop. I could see someone was using a flashlight. The light filtered under the door above the stairs. I decide I better get out of there. I gathered my stuff and climbed out the back door, opening it very slowly and watching with great care as I went out the door. There were two pick-up trucks alongside the house. The vehicles had back lights on in the beds illuminating only the truck beds. I could see three men in the bed of one and two in the bed of the other. I figured there must be four more wandering in the house. I moved off into the woods thinking since it was cold I should not leave tracks or they would be very faint. I moved slowly, watching, waiting a few beats and then moving.

Yes, I had some training at this sort of thing. I followed in my dad's footsteps before school, was a Recon Marine as well. I was born in 1989. I was a late life child for my mom. I had an older brother who was killed in an automobile accident when I was a little boy. I joined the marines at 17. I had been in Afghanistan. My Dad was a young officer, barely out of OCS in the last stages of Vietnam when it started going all wrong for the ARVN Army. He was with ARVN Special Forces when they fought absolutely like tigers trying to save their comrades in the edges of Laos very late in the war. He was evacuated before the fall of Saigon in 1973 at the age of twenty-two. My Dad taught me well. So did the Corps. So yes, I know to move slowly, take my time, slide my feet slowly from one spot to another rather than stepping out and taking the chance of tripping. I am sure of one thing and the guys in the trucks never had any training or discipline applied to them at all. In the house they discovered nothing more than they or someone else had left earlier. They lit the house afire and left.

After the fire burned down by itself I was still tired so I got into the back seat of the car and slept for a while longer. When the sun began to peek through over the horizon I awakened. It was time to make a move and get some distance between me and this place. I found my bearings, kept the sun at my back initially and began to move through the deepest part of the woods, up and down through cuts and even through some deep cuts with a little technical climbing involved. I never saw or heard another human being until late in the day. It was nearing five o' clock in the afternoon when I began to hear cars, a lot of noise and some shooting going on.

The highway seemed to be closer than I had meant it to be so my guess was I had unconsciously veered to the northwest slightly as the highway to Frenchtown went in that direction. Again I began to move very carefully, maintaining cover at all times, but I decided I had to know roughly where I was.

As I slithered to the edge of the woods and took a look at what was in front of me, I found I had covered the distance to the turn off into Frenchtown with no trouble during the day. The exit to Frenchtown was right in front of me. And so were about thirty militiamen. They were heavily armed, all of them. They had a couple out of a car. The man was already dead. The woman was everything but dead. They were still raping her. There was not one thing in the world I could do short of killing her to make her existence any better. I slithered back away from the road block and moved very slowly and very quietly toward the town. I knew I had to go a little east to get to the town and quite a bit east to get around it to head in the direction that would take me to dad's place.

But it was too light, too easy for others to see. As I neared the town a bullet clipped the tree I was standing close to. It was nearing dark and I think the guy missed me because it was coming on dark. But the shot alerted the entire militia group. Frenchtown is like a lot of small forest surrounded towns. It has kind of a perimeter road around it. As I went back into the woods to try and escape I could see pick-up trucks coming around the perimeter road with spotlights on them. Shit. I found a small defile and walked in it for quite a while thinking the depth of it would keep me from being seen. And apparently it did. But apparently some of the locals knew it was there as well.

I heard them well before I saw them. They had flashlights of course. They weren't smart enough to use night vision goggles. I knew if they caught me they would kill me. I didn't want to get into a battle. On the other hand during my walk I had been preparing myself for the possibility I might run onto one or more of their kind and have to fight them. It could not be with a gun, at least not with the guns I had. I moved quietly toward them. They walked noisily down the wash away from me toward what? I didn't know for sure but I guessed the road might join up with the wash. So I decided to move out of the wash. We were all deep enough into the trees now so the spotlights were of no use except to create shadow. Apparently one of them thought he saw my shadow. He unloaded a 30 round clip from what was evidently an AK-47 or AK-74 if it were the later model. He was aiming a good two hundred yards in front of where I was located. None of the rounds he fired threatened me.

I decided if the people looking for me separated at all I would do them quietly and one at a time. They separated. I killed the first one with a thrust of the K-bar into his kidney that paralyzed him and then cut his throat and held him still until he bled out. The other one got nervous and came back toward me. He was easy. I knocked him out with a blow from the AK his buddy had been carrying and then killed him and took off. This time I moved as quickly as I could. Both of them had been carrying nine millimeter Beretta pistols, both of the pistols were silenced. I took them, their knives and all the ammunition I could find on the two of them before I left. I covered them with rocks and leaves as quickly as I could and got out of there. I left their rifles but booby trapped them so they would blow up the next time they were fired if no one looked in the barrel.

I was on the other side of Frenchtown and found the road to my dad's place by the time dawn came around. I don't think anyone discovered the bodies until well after dawn. I found a kind of deadfall of several trees after I started to move toward my dad's place. It was ten miles deep into the forest. I hoped no one in Frenchtown even knew the place existed. It seemed sure to me there were some who must know about the place I hid.

Before going to sleep in the day I made a leafy bed under the deadfall, placed a few rocks in what looked like a haphazard arrangement around the bed I had made to create a defensive position and went to sleep. It was a fitful sleep, not really very restful at all, but it was needed and the time passed. Soon enough it was late afternoon again. I was a hunted man by the time I awakened. There were vehicles going up and down every road in every direction imaginable. I saw them, heard them, watched them shooting at shadows in the dusk, watched them drinking, screaming they were going to kill me. They had found their brethren and they were mad as hell.

As soon as it was full dark I began to move again. I had eaten some canned vegetables, wished that I had some chicken or a good cut of prime rib of beef, something meaty and solid. But I might never be able to have meat like prime rib again except and unless it was deer or elk. As I went through the woods I found several small streams and filled a couple of bottles with water.

I had some purifying tablets that I always carried with me if I had my K-Bar. They were in the handle, along with matches, a flint and needle and thread. So hydration was not my problem. I just wanted a good, hot, filling meal for a change. If I got to my dad's maybe it could happen. He would be sure to have stockpiled food enough for all of us I imagined.

As I paralleled the road toward my dad's place I wondered if the militiamen had found it. If they had it would have taken a lot more than four of them to get him down. The trail, if it could be called a trail, which went toward his home was an up and down affair, all dirt, and as a result of the traffic on the road there was a lot of dirt in the air. It made traveling in the forest even more difficult than normally.

Of course as soon as it was full dark the searchers had their spot-lights on, their headlights on their special K.C. Hi-lighters on as well. I moved even more slowly then, moved even further back away from the faint trail and almost fell off a cliff at one point as a result of the overall miasma that was created by the pick-up trucks, the dust and their lights. At one point I was not entirely sure of what was going on or where I was. It was a total mess. But somehow I kept going, kept getting further away from the town, kept on walking slowly, making progress, seeing less of the pick-up trucks, hearing less of the voices and shooting.

It became evident they had no idea where my dad lived as I got further into the forest. Of course the track of the trail, which I felt more comfortable in staying close to as the traffic decreased to nothing, was little more than an animal trail. He must have another way in and out I thought. And knowing my Dad it had to be, I had to be right, there had to be another way. It was his way to see to it he had escape avenues that no one aside from my Dad would know about.

The dawn came and I began to look for a shelter in which I could hide. I found a copse of trees, rocks and rubble nature had deposited in one or more of its torrential downpours. There were felled trees here and there and I was able to gather enough pine needles and pine boughs to make a fairly comfortable bed once my coat was laid over the top of the natural material. I was asleep in no time.

The daytime belonged to the militiamen in those early days. They were a bunch of incompetents when it came to finding someone who didn't want to be found. In terms of noise discipline they were totally incompetent. They made a lot of noise and woke me up a couple of times. I looked around carefully and saw nothing, listened and heard them at a long distance. They had lost the thread of the trail. They had no training and no one to track me apparently. Or at least they had no one competent to track me. There was no way for them to use dogs because dogs need some kind of scent to work from. The earth is full of scents. If dogs can pick one out they can track anything. If they do not have one scent to trail then they cannot trail well at all.

So I slept. And I awakened again late in the afternoon when the lighting in my makeshift bedroom changed from bright to gray. There was no movement around me, there were no trucks running around through the trees with men shooting at anything. Nonetheless I waited until it was nearly full dark before I picked up my stuff, rearranged my pack and went on my way. The only thing I really had to worry about now was whether they had set any deadfalls or other forms of traps for me including perhaps the larger steel jawed traps used for large forest animals such as bears, wolves, etc.

But since the track seemed clear of traffic now I decided to stay several yards inside the trees and just off the beaten path, what little beaten path there was. It was a smart move on my part for at one place I spotted a deadfall in the middle of the road. In another place I spotted a trap that would have impaled me on a tree like those that the Vietcong had used in South Vietnam. That one, I thought, probably was put there by my father. It made me even more alert which caused me to spot the glint of wire in the little moonlight there was and to avoid the trip wire that would have put me into a net. By then I thought I must be getting close to my dad's place. And lo and behold, less than half an hour later I heard a man say to me in a gruff, marine voice, "What the hell took you so long? I heard you coming at least for the last two miles!"

I had to laugh. He did too. We embraced, laughed a little and he asked what all the noise was with the pick-ups running around in the trees. I said they were looking for me. He asked why and I said "Well a couple of nights ago I had to kill two of theirs."

"That couldn't have been any challenge," he responded. "Those bastards are totally incompetent. They have some kind of encampment down near town. It is just off the circular drive that runs around town. Did you see their camp?"

"Yeah. I ran onto their roadblock out on Hwy. 93. They had a couple of pilgrims out there. One they had already killed. The woman they were dallying with before killing her. I found a little gully kind of a deal running away from the town. A couple of them guessed I might take it and came along with rifles, flashlights, what have you. They were trying to stay in the dark and got a little ways apart. I killed one and then the other. I took their gear except for the rifles. I already had this one so I just took the pistols and their ammo for the pistols. I think they found them two mornings ago. Since then I have been moving very slowly in your direction."

"It's good to see you, son. Why didn't you just drive up here?"

"Dad, I got stopped at a roadblock out near Idaho Falls. They warned me there might be militia groups. After I got some gas in Missoula and ate something, the most expensive hamburgers I ever had I think, I started out of town and as I was coming to 93 something made me pull off the road. I found a house where I thought I might be able to talk to someone about what was going on in the area. I found a couple who had been tortured and shot. He was an ex-cop from San Diego I think."

My dad shook his head and said "Yeah, he and his wife were really nice people. His name was Charley and she was Berneice."

"They had been dead at least a day or so. I put them into their shed. I found some food and some clothes and then found a little private storage place he had for his rifle and shotgun. I got those out of there, found his .45 pistol and some spare ammunition. I packed up what food I could find and put together enough stuff to be able to get here on foot. Then I ran onto the roadblock. I was on foot and they didn't see me there. One of them apparently saw me just before dark near Frenchtown. He took a shot at me and missed by about a foot."

"Careless, son, careless. You know better. You must have silhouetted yourself.. Your sergeants and officers trained you better. So did I."

"I know, dad. Have you been watching T.V. at all?"

"Not since after Ruthie and the kids arrived, Will. We have been having so much fun we didn't need a television. It was good to have it off in fact. I didn't miss it a damn bit. Both the boys have been doing some plinking with a .22 rifle of mine but in the basement where it could not be heard. Once I saw the spotlights and heard all the crap down on the roads I thought something bad had to be going on. But hell no we have not seen the T.V. in over a week."

"Then you don't know."

"Don't know what?"

"We are at war, dad. We have been at war with Russia and maybe some others now for over a week. There have been some nuclear exchanges. The eastern part of Montana, the Dakotas got hit, as did Omaha. I was told Omaha was obliterated. I don't know about the east coast but the west coast was not involved the last I heard. Do you have electric power?"

"War? How can that be? What happened? Yes, son, we have electrical power from our own generator. That is all we have ever had. And we have a satellite dish. We can take a look at what is going on with the dish and see if anything is being broadcast."

"Well we might be able to get something from the west coast. Again I don't know about the east coast. And I don't know about Colorado either. What I do know is civil order has broken down here in Montana and in Idaho. The militias have taken over, dad. The cops won't even go outside compounds in the night. The side roads like 93 are being patrolled only by militias. One more thing. The cops told me down near Idaho Falls if I tried to go beyond Missoula to Kellogg, for instance, they wouldn't allow me to go there. I don't know what it has to do with anything. But I think if we are all going to go to the west coast we will have to walk a long distance."

"Well, son, maybe we ought to eliminate some of the enemy, make it a bit easier to take the roads. I see you have gathered a couple of silenced weapons. As you know I have been putting together weapons and ammunition for a long time. One of those weapons is a Heckler & Koch MP-5 machine rifle which will fire bursts, single shot or full automatic. It has a silencer on it as well. Do you think it's possible for us to get close to that roadblock?"

"It's quite a ways back there, dad."

"I didn't ask how far it was son. It is not so far as you think. Not the way we would go."

"And how would that be?"

"I have a car here. We can drive most of the way without any fear of being detected. But hell we wouldn't need to drive. I have plenty of gasoline and I would love to put a little fear in those bastards who think they can ride roughshod over the public in general. I was a military man for a lot of years, son. And I put those years in for one reason. I believed in our system of government. I still do. Those bastards are trying to end our way of government and our way of life and establish some kind of military rule in this area. I don't think I want that to happen. Are you with me, son?"

Now how in the hell could I ever have said no to my father after a speech like he had just made? As we walked up to the door of the house I said "Sure, dad, but let's see if we can do this with a minimum of chance they will understand who is doing it and how to get at us."

"Exactly what I have in mind son, exactly what I have in mind. But of course we won't mention this to the women, will we?"

Again I had no answer but yes. Ah but you might thing we are crazy. Who are we, my father and I, to take on a large group of militia people? I mean he is 72 years old. Oh yeah? After the Marine Corps my father stayed in excellent physical condition. His weight was actually less than what it had been when he was twenty. For a number of years he has worked hard on the house. He may be stronger than I am. He is as lean and tough as any man alive in his age bracket. And his age bracket, though typical of "senior citizens" could easily have been thirty to forty years of age. He is a formidable man indeed.

So is it a dumb idea for us to see what we can do to eliminate some of those murderers, those self-styled militiamen. If we had no training, oh but we do; if we had not maintained physical abilities, oh but we have; it might be a dumb idea. If we think it is becoming a bad idea, a dumb idea, we can always retreat and defend our little fortress. Hell they don't even know where we are. So for now, no it is not a dumb idea.

Chapter 3

Home

Then we were home, my wife was in my arms and my kids were all over me. God it was so good to see them, to be with them again. I really had wondered in the last several days whether it might ever be able to be true again. No one really asked me any questions right away about why I had a rifle, a shotgun, three pistols, a whole backpack partially filled with canned goods as well as a sack with some empty and some full cans. I filled up the hall closet with all the stuff except for the canned goods which I gave to my mother.

Mom is a very sweet and very patient woman, but she is also the wife of a Recon Marine. And she has weathered two men in her family going to war and surviving in the most brutal and dangerous jobs imaginable. After she kissed me on the cheek and hugged me in turn she waited for me to have time for the wife and kids for a moment, watched me unload, and then said to me,

"It's so wonderful to have you home, son. Come into the living room and sit down so we can all talk together in a few, okay?"

Marching orders is what she meant. She wanted to know what the hell was going on causing me to be armed to the teeth. She could see I had what could only be blood stains on my clothing (which she took off me to the laundry room right away), and a bunch of canned goods. She took the canned goods to the kitchen and put them away. She noted one particular brand of Kipper Snacks was the kind which Charley and Berneice loved. She went back to the closet where I had hung the Sam Browne I was wearing and looked at it for a moment. Written on the inside of the belt, something I had not noticed, in a kind of leather embroidery, was the word Chas.

She stood at the closet door and cried silently for a moment, wiped her tears and then came into the living room and waited for everyone to calm down a little in the living room. When everyone was seated and dad had his pipe lit up I said to Ruthie, "Honey, would you please turn on the television and see if you can find any stations broadcasting." There were none. "Dad, do you have a radio that we could try." He tuned his stereo to AM/FM, selected FM and went across the band, nothing. Then he tuned it to AM and went across the band. He found one channel open but just static. He left it on and sat back down. He just nodded to me.

"I am so sorry to have to tell you this. The U.S. is at war with Russia." There were gasps, Ruthie started to cry, my boys gathered at her side and hugged her, my mother leaked a few tears and sat down next to dad, taking his hand in hers. I waited for a couple of minutes until everyone had calmed down a little and said "There have been some nuclear exchanges." Again the gasps and the crying. "I don't really know how many. I took off from D.C. more than a week ago to get here. On my third day of travel I was between Omaha and Cheyenne when I saw what appeared to be at least three nuclear explosions near

Omaha. Later I heard that Omaha was gone. Still later on outside Idaho Falls I heard eastern Montana and the Dakotas had also been hit. I assumed the strikes on Montana and the Dakotas meant Colorado had been hit and D.C. probably had been hit as well. It's about as much as I can tell you about the current situation as far as the war with Russia is concerned. It all started with North Korea trying to hit us and then a whole series of world wide blunders kept coming up. I saw the handwriting on the wall when I got you guys over here and took off myself."

My youngest son, Will, who is now nine years old, asked me, "Does this mean you will have to go to war, dad? Or you, grandpa?" He looked at my dad who just shook his head.

"No, son," I said. "No, I don't think so. But there are some things we may have to do which will be a little bit like war, your grandpa and I."

My mom chimed in and said, "Why do you have Charlie's Sam Browne? Are they gone?"

"Yes, mom. Charley and Berneice will not be visiting again any time soon." I nodded to her as tears began to run down her face. She got up and went into the kitchen and came back out with a plate of cookies and a large jar of milk. We all took some and sat and wondered quietly what life would bring us in the next few what, days, weeks, months, years? Would there be years left for any of us? God what a thought. I put the thought away about the time the radio blared.

"This is Radio United States. Please stay in your homes. Please do not panic. The United States has been attacked. We have responded. The nuclear war is over. We need your help. The best way you can help now is to stay in your homes. We will broadcast every hour with this message. God Bless you all and God Bless these United States of America."

Dad decided it was time for him to contribute something to the discussion after the radio broadcast. Everyone was kind of babbling at each other, wondering what the hell was going on. He and I were the only ones with a grasp on reality and even he only knew what I told him. He said, "We have taken a blow before and prevailed. We will do so again. We have work to do. Come on Gene, Billy, and you too son, we have some work to do on the outside of the place. You ladies get some grub up for us if you will please. This will be hungry work. Okay boys, son, let's get with it."

We went outside and he opened a door that I would not have known was there. He opened it and inside was a generator running fairly quietly. I saw an exhaust running out of the generator and asked, "Where does the heat come out, dad?" He knew why I was asking. If the militia boys were smart enough or capable enough to do what they had done already there was probably a helicopter pilot among them. And if it were true it would be simple for a helicopter to investigate, discover and fire missiles at a heat plume from the exhaust from a generator. We, Dad and I both, had seen a lot of dead men whose only mistake in hiding themselves had been to make a fire or to dig a hole and put a fire in it which vented straight out into the air.

"Don't worry, son. I vented it into the rock of the mountainside below us on the other side of the house a long time ago." He walked me over to the edge of what was a deep chasm behind the house. It had what appeared to be a very faint animal trail leading down its steep sides. He said, "About fifty feet down there is a large open cave. I have it camouflaged now and it is where the exhaust comes out. I am sure there is a little that leaks out the front of the cave but it is all bedrock and would give the appearance of radiating the heat of the day off rock. But here is what we have to deal with." He had put a railing up around the back of the house to make sure the kids and anyone else going back there was safe.

He began to pull it out of the ground. We had most of it out and laid down on the ground within minutes. It was a good thing. As we were finishing covering the lines of the railings we began to hear a helicopter. We covered ourselves and sent the boys back inside. Dad had created a small natural looking shooting spot. We watched the helicopter fly directly over us without seeing us. We watched it do a grid search of the area without seeing dad's home. Amazing. Dad said, "I flew over this place a lot of years ago now, Will, and it was nothing but rocky ground. It took me a long time to begin to develop it. I used the rock in the walls and ceilings, covered it with the local soil from areas away from here, places where the soil would not be missed particularly. I covered the entire place with the soil to a depth of nearly six inches. The doors I put in and painted or covered as well. The windows open electrically. Everything is electrically operated so you know. Some of them open only into firing slits behind rock and dirt as well as a four inch steel plate that protects the shooter. Later I will show you the entries into the cave below. That is our refrigerator and our storage area. It is where our fuel is located. Anyone that wants to get there has to go through the house. To go down the pathway would take a technical climber."

"Jesus, dad, this place is a fortress."

"You are right, son, but any fortress can be breached. It is one of the first lessons of warfare. You already know about those maxims. But it would be hard to take this place. It could withstand a five hundred pound bomb I think. Anyway, here." He handed me a plan. It was a plan of firing areas outside the house. They were all connected by tunnels.

He opened the entry into the tunnel and went down into it. Next to the opening was a flashlight.

The tunnel was not tall enough to stand upright but it was not uncomfortable to move in there either. There was rock over our head. As we walked along he said "This was a bitch of a project. I am only going to take you to one of the other firing points. They are like spider holes but the top does not have to be removed in order to fire out of them." We came to the spot in a few more steps and came up out of the ground there.

On the plan there were other indications. I saw a rope sign and asked, "Is this the rope catchment that I ran onto?"

"Yes. And the pit you found is a way behind that, you see the P."

"Yes and the tree trap is back there as well, and I see the T."

"What you never did see but I am sure you would have if you had stayed closer to the trail, is the punji stake traps. There are five of them and you narrowly avoided the first one. Each is fitted with a sound device that registers footfalls kind of like those that the Border Patrol uses along the border. They don't always work well but the punji stakes would if someone was stupid enough to walk on the trail. There are also several mines placed along the trail at intervals. You spotted one of the trip wires that would set one of them off. As you progressed down the area of the pathway, I watched you on the cameras which are night vision capable. They are mounted in some of the trees. I was proud of how you were able to negotiate your way through all the traps I set for anyone. Of course I would have disabled them if I thought you couldn't do it but I saw no reason to doubt you."

I laughed my butt off and then finally said, as he grinned at me, "Damn, dad, I am sure glad you had confidence in me." He got it and smiled and we went back to the house. He told the kids they would have to stay inside now unless they were escorted outside. He told them he had some things set up that could be dangerous to them and wanted them to be with him or me if they wanted to go out. He told Ruthie the same thing.

He turned to mom after talking to Ruthie and the kids and said "We are going to have to become a little more energy conscious now, honey. And our cooking will have to be limited to the convection oven for a while I'm afraid."

She smiled knowingly at him and said, "Is there a danger to us like there was for Charley and Berneice?"

My dad turned to me. I answered. "I'm afraid there is, mom. And it's going to last a while, unless dad and I can eliminate its source."

Ruthie, my lovely wife of twelve years, entered into the conversation then. She looked directly at me and said "I think it's time you told us what happened to Charley and Berneice, Will."

"Are the kids somewhere they cannot hear?" She nodded. "When I found Charley and Berneice they had been gone for at least twenty-four hours. They were tortured before they were killed. My guess is Berneice was repeatedly raped before she was killed. She and Charley were both badly cut up and then they were shot."

My dad said "That could be those kids from Frenchtown we have heard are so problematical, honey. Remember they used to come and harass Charley a lot while he was working around the place."

"Well, dad, whoever they are, whatever kind of people they are, they are apparently in control of the roads and the town now. There are dozens of them running around in pick-up trucks shooting at anything moving. Charley and Berneice are not the only ones they have killed. I watched them for a very short time with a couple on the highway who just happened to be driving this way. It was sad but I had to get here. The only thing I could have done is kill her. But here I am now, and I think dad and I can do something about this mess if we can get close enough to them."

"Can you still run, son?" my dad asked me.

"Yes I think so. Not sure how far. But certainly several miles at a jog at least."

"That is plenty. From the way you described the roadblock it actually is only about two miles from here as the crow flies. The terrain is difficult to walk or run but it's not far. Tomorrow we will do a little recon. But tonight we all need to get some rest and talk amongst ourselves about this whole thing."

We all had a good dinner, listened to another broadcast of the Radio United States station which gave no new information, sat around and either moped or chatted quietly the rest of the evening until around nine o' clock in the evening when we all went to bed. The house was solid, insulated from room to room; each room had its own vents for the systems of cooling and heating.

The cooling was low, creating a lulling kind of air flow. My wife and I made love with each other quietly and peacefully for the first time in several weeks. We didn't talk much. We kissed a lot, said I love you a lot and held each other before, during and after. For her I'm sure it was a frightening evening despite my "coming home." We slept hard. At first we were entwined in each other's arms, then spooned, through most of the night.

The next morning dad knocked on the door early. I got up, told Ruthie to go back to sleep for a while. I went out into the hallway in underwear. He handed me forest camos. We dressed, covered our skin with forest camo dressings, gloves and covers over our shoes. We covered our weapons. He had camo web gear and vests which we donned.

He handed me a holster for the nine millimeter silenced pistol I had taken from one of the two idiots I had killed earlier. He already was wearing the other. He handed me night vision goggles and a marine cap.

He handed me an MP-5 automatic rifle that had a long silencer on the end of its barrel as well. We took knives in case we needed them or the contents of their handles. We took extra ammunition and clips. We were both carrying more than two hundred fifty rounds each. That sounds like a lot but it can be expended in a firefight in a very short time. We left the house with no conversation necessary, no signals, no need for anything except reliance on each other. We jogged away from the house with him leading.

An hour or so later, still full dark, we stopped. I had been hearing the idiots for a long time. They had a huge fire going next to the road. There were four of them. There were five cars along side the road. All of the cars had at least two bodies in them. One had two adults and three children, all dead. We crept along the length of the line of cars they had created for us to use as cover. We went slowly.

One of them wandered off into the woods toward us to take a leak. I peeled off and went with him for a moment. As he pulled his pants down, I killed him. It was simple and fast. I slung his M-16 over my back, took all his ammo along with his pistol which was similar to the one I was carrying. I took his knife as well. I went back to dad. He made the sign for three. We crept forward to the edge of the car. I took the one on the right. Dad took the one in the center. Both of them took a nine millimeter bullet in the center of the forehead. The other guy jumped up, looked around and fell dead as dad shot him.

If this all seems a little cold-blooded, it was. But remember there were thirteen bodies in cars along the road. We thought these criminals deserved nothing better and it was clear the "law" that had existed no longer did, or at best was ineffective. There were no cops, there was no army in the area except for the two marines who had just blooded these militia murderers. Difficult times make difficult tasks into commonplace occurrences. Dad and I both learned the lessons of recon marines, including doing those things necessary.

We went to them, stripped them of their weapons and knives, took what little food they were carrying in their trucks, booby trapped the trucks to blow with Semtex covered in an arc with ball bearings. We hoped the militiamen would come, see the dead, decide to take their trucks without looking closely at them and start them up with at least two on board. Each of those two would die as well. We melted back into the forest and waited. Just as dawn started to break in the forest behind us two more trucks came along with four more guys.

We watched. They got out, looked at their partners, decided what they needed to do and two of them got into the trucks their partners had brought out to the roadblock. They died as they turned the ignition switches. The other two dropped where they stood. We ran down and took their weapons and then made a hasty exit into the forest at a dead run.

We were within a half a mile of the house when we heard the helicopter. We buried up and waited. It flew over us and went on its way. So did we. Before it came back we made it back to the house. It was a grim start but a successful one at the least. We now had six more rifles and pistols, several more knives and some additional food. Not a bad night's work. Neither Ruthie nor my mom asked us anything about what we had done in those early morning hours. We never volunteered anything about it either. Dad and I cleaned up, ate breakfast and played with the kids for most of the day. We all went to bed early.

After we were in bed Ruthie said "What happened this morning?"

"Ruthie this area is a war zone involving militiamen who are killing civilians. We are now at war with them. We did what we had to do. It was a start?" She let the realities pass.

Attack when the enemy is unprepared.
Appear where you are not expected.
Sun Tzu, The Art of War

Chapter 4

War at home, how long will it last?

We could hear them out there, the helicopter, the blaring horns of the truck, the rounds being loosed into the shadows of trees and the trees themselves. Dad and I went from one spider hole to another looking for anyone coming close to the property. Luckily none of them figured the "animal trail" which ended at the house was really a road. None of them but one.

This guy was apparently smarter than the rest of them, and he went for a walk up the road by himself. Dad's traps didn't get him. The guy just kept on coming. We saw him for a long time. Dad's cameras were working very well indeed. He had a hand held radio attached to his belt, and he had one of those shoulder epaulet mounted microphones that he could reach up and key while doing something else as well. I could hear chatter on the radio from the station that I finally took up that was within feet of the area through which he would pass before seeing the house itself, if he could figure out what it was. He kept coming.

It was getting dark fast. I expected the guy to turn around and head back but something kept him coming. As he passed by me I opened the portal of the spider hole quietly and stepped up behind him. He must have felt my presence at the last second. He started to turn as I plunged my K-Bar into his kidney. I twisted it and he gurgled and sank to his knees. I finished him, took his equipment and his radio and threw him over the cliff. He fell a long way.

I heard the helicopter coming, heard someone on the radio calling for someone called M-5 who didn't answer. I guessed it might be the guy I just threw over the cliff. I slipped back into the spider hole and headed back through the tunnels to the house. The helicopter came over the area several times and then settled on the cliff side. I heard over the radio which I had turned down low and was using an ear bud that was attached to it, "M-5 appears to have fallen off a cliff the dumb shit."

"Call off the search then, the helicopter can return to base. This is M-1, out." The guy who identified himself as M-1 then came back on the radio. I recognized his voice at that point. He called for M-22. There was an answer and then M-1 said, "M-5 is gone. How many do we have on the blocks this evening?"

M-22 or someone who identified themselves as M-22 said "Twelve, six at each location."

M-1 answered "10-4, out."

When I got back to the house, I asked dad where he thought the second "block" might be and he guessed it would be on the other side of town on Hwy. 93. We discussed how we could attack the place they called the blocks and he said it was a long trek at the best and even longer back. It would require some wheels. So then I asked "Where do you think the headquarters will be?"

"I have no doubt that it will be at the police station in town or maybe the State Patrol office if they were able to take those boys out."

"Well it's probably too soon to think about taking the police station or State Patrol Office out. I am guessing completely about their numbers but I think they have about thirty or more in their group. One of them called M-22 on the radio gives me that number for now. Do you think they are smart enough to organize a rapid response team?"

"Son, I would think anyone would be smart enough after what we did to them last night. We took out eight of their finest and one more this evening so far. But even if they have a rapid response team we can do something different tonight if that strikes your fancy."

"What would that be, dad?"

"Here's what I have in mind, son." He outlined a basic plan, and I have to admit the old man is diabolical when he puts his mind to something. We got geared up, left the ladies with our love and headed out pretty much in the same fashion as the night before, and we were headed to the same roadblock as the night before as well.

When we got to the area of the roadblock we began to slither and crawl. We thought they might post a couple of sentries in the forest. Actually they posted four. The six guys at the block were two on the road and four in the woods. I took care of two of those in the woods and the old man took care of two as well. He was forced to use the silenced pistol on the second one when the first made more noise than he should have.

The two guys at the road block began to stir around when they heard that sound, a strange kind of noise. One of them said "What should we do?" Those were his last words. I shot him in the forehead as dad shot the other one. We cleaned up their weapons, radios and food again, stacked their bodies in their trucks this time and lit the trucks afire then headed home. Six more down!

Obviously they couldn't continue to take losses at that rate and be viable as a group. We wondered if the deaths of so many, twelve already, might have chased any of them off. We would not know whether it was true for many months to come. We had, it turned out, only just begun.

Among the weapons that we were able to garner from the militiamen this time were some RPG's made in Russia, or China or maybe in Czechoslovakia. There were two launchers and half a dozen rocket propelled grenades. Since we had booby trapped their weapons in the past we didn't want to fire any of the weapons we had confiscated until we broke them down, checked them out and looked for any destructive devices that might be planted in them. It was good that we took the time to check them out..

The warheads of two of the rocket propelled grenades were set to explode on ignition of the launcher. Who ever fired these babies was going to have his own personal fireworks show for a flashing moment of surprise. But we were able to reset them and eliminate the danger. All the rifles we had taken away from the militiamen were brand spanking new military K-Bar (extra strong barrel for extended usage at a high rate of fire) barrels.

They were able to be fired at burst, single shot or full automatic rate. They could only have come from a military base or a police barracks. The weapons told us that the State Police barracks in Frenchtown was gone and the men, the several State Police that resided there probably had been murdered. The weapons also told us the militiamen might have taken over a National Guard weapons cache in the next town up the road. Many of the locals had served the nation as National Guardsmen. It could mean we would begin to find men opposing us who were trained or it could mean that they were all dead or captive.

We had to have some information. We decided on our next sortie we had to take at least one prisoner. We had some fun with the kids that morning and then went to sleep. We woke up at mom's urging about 4:30 in the afternoon. It would not be dark for several hours but she wanted us all to have a nice dinner together for a change.

Mom is not a religious woman, but that night she had set a beautiful table with a nice piece of ham, one of the last of those she had frozen, and a full course meal of salad, frozen vegetables that tasted nearly as good as fresh, and a small cake just the right size for all of us. As we sat down she asked for us all to be grateful to God for our gift of food and then said, "Dear God, our family wants to survive, wants to continue to help create this wonderful nation we have been for so long now. But God, for us to do those things our men must engage in war. You know those needs as well as they do. Give them your strength Lord, the humility to live in peace and the ability to understand the needs of their work without self loathing. Thank you God for this family and all we do in your name. Amen"

The work that dad and I were doing was certainly not "God's" work. But it was necessary if we were all to survive. It was also necessary if some reasonable sense of who we were as a nation was to be restored. In the night, just after dusk we began again. We decided that the roadblock had to be our focus for several sorties until they made it such a strong point we could not overcome the odds. We ran as far as we dared and then began to crawl and sneak toward our evening's rendezvous. Once again they had posted sentries in the darkness of the forest.

The forest was our domain. We ruled the night and the forest. Six of them died in the night in the forest. Then we went to the roadblock. This night they had an additional four on the trucks. They also had murdered some that were driving on the highway again. Among those dead in the cars next to the road were several young children. It was sickening to me to see what those bastards did to those children. In the name of what, I wondered. Anarchy was what they seemed to prefer. Death was what we would give them.

Most military men who are trained at all will sit in the dark, move as little as possible when they know they are in danger, let the other guy make the mistakes in the night. These men, young, virile, strong, but untrained were no match for trained military men. We shot three of them in the forehead. The fourth hid. We snuck up close to him, made a noise, he looked up to see what it was and I knocked him out with a sap.

We carried him far enough back into the forest so that we could interrogate him without interference if another group of his buddies came along. Dad stayed in the background to act as a guard for both of us and so he would not be seen and give away our numbers if we decided to let this kid go.

I gagged him and showed him my knife. I made a small incision in his nostril. It bled a lot. He tried to yell but I sapped him again. He awoke, groggy, not knowing what his circumstances were for sure and looked around. He saw me and began to cringe. I showed him my knife again and put it close to his right eye. He shook his head violently side to side. I said to him, "If I take the gag out of your mouth you cannot yell. Do you hear me clearly?"

He nodded. I took the gag out. He opened his mouth wide as if to yell. I sapped him again, not enough to take him completely out, just enough to stun him and make him understand. As he came around I put my knife in front of his face again. He understood. He didn't start to yell again. He sat quietly. I said to him, "How many are in your group?"

He said, "I don't know for sure. I am called M-45 in the group. I think they give us numbers that go with the numbers of the group."

I asked him, "What is the highest number you know of in your group?"

"One of the guys that was here tonight was number 56 I think. I have not heard any numbers higher than that."

"Do you know how many of your group have died in the last few days?"

"No but I know there have been a lot of them. One of them was a low number, number 5, I think. He is the brother of our leader. Our leader is so mad about it he wants to light the entire forest afire in order to smoke you guys out."

"Where did you guys get the M-16 rifles you had tonight?"

"The barracks up the road where the National Guard was. They just opened the doors and let us have whatever we wanted. They didn't want to fight us."

"Do you have mortars?"

"I don't know what a mortar is, sir."

"It's a long tube that mounts on a base plate. You drop a shell down it and the shell fires off, and explodes somewhere down the line." I said.

"No. Not that I know of. We have some machine guns on the helicopter now, but other than those I don't know of anything heavier than the rifles. Hell we don't need em," he laughed. "Most people are so stupid they stop at our roadblocks, we shoot the men right away, have some fun with the women and kids and then shoot them too."

"Why are you killing those people?"

"Well you know, they are outsiders. And they have gas in their cars. And most of them are carrying a lot of money. We siphon off the gas and junk their cars unless they are pick-ups or vans and of course we keep any weapons they may have and their money."

"How many have you killed, son?"

"Well, I just helped to do what we have out there right now. We only got two cars in this afternoon and evening."

We had looked earlier and there were four women in one of the cars. It was evident they were about college age girls. They were completely naked, had been badly cut up and tortured before they died. All had evidently been raped. I asked him about the girls. "Did you enjoy the girls, boy? Ever have any so tight before?"

"Oh boy were they ever," he said and then got a look of surprise on his face. "You tricked me." After I talked a little further with the boy I took him back to his truck, the one we had taken him out of after killing the other three in the truck. "Is this your truck boy?"

"Well it's the one the boss gave me, but I think I get to keep it from now on, yeah." He was smiling and happy to be back with his buds and his truck.

We had already stripped the weapons, the cash, the ammunition and the food and drinks they had. I tied his hands to the wheel of the truck with duct tape. He had a small Buck knife on the side of his belt. I opened it and put it in his right hand. I told him "After we leave you can work yourself loose and go back to town. We don't need you any longer."

We had set the truck up the same as the first two with a small amount of Semtex sitting right under the driver's seat. We took off. A few minutes later we heard the explosion and saw a fire ball go into the sky. We knew what it was from. If he'd had any sense at all he would have cut himself free and got out of the truck and ran back to town. He didn't have any sense, nor any time left. Another ten were gone from this group of murderers.

As we walked back toward the house, moving slowly again, we began to see some vehicles coming from the direction of Missoula. We snuck out to the edge of the highway and watched as a number of army trucks rolled by. But they were being driven by people who were not dressed in military gear. Some of them had twin fifties mounted on top. Most appeared to be unarmed.

They were widely separated like a normal military convoy would be. There would be a jeep at the end with the second in command of the group in the vehicle. We set up with the MP-5's on burst. When the Jeep came even with us we shot both the driver and the passengers. There were three of them in the jeep. After that as we walked back into the trees we could hear the radio again, "M-3, come in M-3. Where are you, M-3?" I wanted to key the radio I had and say "He's dead." But I didn't!

As we wended our way home the helicopter passed over us several times. We were totally covered, had donned firefighter's silver fire repellant blankets in addition to our clothing so we could present the smallest possible heat signature in addition to being as invisible as was possible. At one point the helicopter turned after it passed by us, flew faster toward us again as we stood behind trees and rocks and fired a machine gun into the forest. But it was firing a good two or three hundred yards beyond where we were located. It must have seen something flare on the infrared or downward looking "Fleer" device in the helicopter and took it as a target. We moved more quickly out of the area as the helicopter hovered and continued to fire in the area behind us.

Then we heard a faint voice on the radio say "Cease firing, cease firing. This is M-7, cease firing. You have hit me already. I am badly wounded. You will need to get me help as soon as possible." We kept on trucking and made it back to the house safely while listening to the radio chatter about M-7. But it shook both of us a little.

We wondered if someone had brought night vision, had followed our trail, or if we were leaving a trail, or if something had keyed them to our area. We looked through the weapons we had confiscated and the ammunition. We found a tracker and smashed it well before arriving back at the house. Damn, I thought, these people are beginning to piss me off. They are getting a little smarter about this little war we are fighting.

That night was not done by the time dad and I got home. It was starry and clear, a beautiful and cool fall Montana night. I sat outside with my oldest boy Gene for a little while and we talked about the stars a little. We used to sit on the roof at home and try to identify them. We were doing the same thing and just enjoying being together. I had one of their radios on with an ear bud in so Gene could not hear what was coming over the radio.

About three hours after we got home I heard on the radio "This is M-1. I don't know who you are but you have now killed over twenty of my men. We are at war, you and I, and I mean to kill you and everyone you love. Know my intent. Know that I will find you people and when I do I will enjoy torturing each one of you before you die." Dad came out and sat down with Gene and I right after the broadcast. Gene was busy counting stars.

Dad asked me "Did you hear the guy who calls himself M-1?"

"Yeah, dad. I guess we cannot expect anything less can we. They have taken some casualties and lost equipment as well as money. He has to be furious with his men and even more so with us."

Gene saw his Grampa, gave him a big hug and said "Grampa are all those people in town bad people? Gramma says she doesn't think all of them are bad. Are they?"

"Gene, I doubt if all the people in the town are bad people. But some are, son, and they are doing bad things. So we are going to see if we can't stop them from doing bad things. What do you think? Is it okay with you if we stop them?"

"It sounds good to me Grampa." And off he went. Of course as much as he loves his Grampa he would think any words coming out of Grampa's mouth would be just fine. I think probably Grampa feels pretty much the same about him.

When Gene had gone back into the house dad and I sat out a little longer. He had a little monitor for the cameras he had in the trees and for the sound devices he had planted some one thousand yards away from the house. All of a sudden, from one area of the sound detector field a lot of activity started. We watched the cameras for a moment before going back into the house. We saw several men walking back and forth in the trees and they were using night vision. We armed up and went into the tunnel system to see what was going to happen.

Each of the men we could see from the cameras were carrying SAW weapons (Squad Automatic Weapon). Apparently they had somehow found a trail leading toward the house, and they were following it. We watched as the lead guy stepped into a punji stake hole and was put out of action. Then another did the same thing. Neither of them were on the radio which apparently had different frequencies than those we had been monitoring. The third guy didn't know what the hell to do. He took off his night goggles. He was maybe fifteen feet from our spider hole when I shot him. He was frantically calling for help on the radio but no one was answering.

Again we took their weapons, stripped and cleaned them, found one tracker and crushed it, found a tracker on each of the guys and crushed them before they went over the edge of the cliffs. They each had thousands of dollars on them. We took their money and everything else of any use including the night vision units and the radios. Dad repaired the damage to his camouflaged covers for the punji stake holes while I was taking the bodies to the cliff.

We equipped three spider holes with SAW weapons. Each of them had been carrying one extra canister with them. Dad took one of them apart the next day and began the process of making more through reverse engineering with some aluminum he had on hand as well as with his wire feed welder. Before the end of the morning we had three more canisters which we filled with belts of ammo we had taken off the others we had killed.

The men we had encountered and dispatched seemed to be carrying a lot of MRE packets. So we had begun to gather quite a supply of MRE's (Meals Ready to Eat) and they were all brand new. We thought it likely they came out of the armory up the road.

The events of the night seemed to make it imperative we adults all sit down and see if we could come to some conclusion about staying for a while, leaving right away, where we would go if we could, all kinds of options which might be available to us. We started the discussion in the late morning after dad and I awakened to the sound of Radio United States. "To all citizens. There has been an invasion of the United States soil for the first time since 1812. We are asking all able bodied men to join our military now!"

This message repeated several times, then the station went off the air. We kept one of each type of the radios we had captured from the militiamen on at all times now. Just after the RUSA announcements the voice came on that had previously identified himself as M-1.

And he said "This is M-1. You heard em soldier boys, whoever the hell you are. Why don't you go enlist? Then we can all live in peace for a time anyway."

He had broadcast on both radios this time. After a pause he said "We would guarantee your safe passage out of this place and good riddance to you. But this offer is only open for the next 24 hours."

What he said put an alteration into our family discussion right away. Dad and I both told the women we could not trust the militiamen under any circumstance. We had not discussed their atrocities before then with mom or Ruthie, but we did now. Ruthie said "Surely there must be some humanity left in those people."

I told her "One of the boys that we came on last night we left for interrogation. I talked to him about fifteen minutes. The last question I asked him was a question to bait him about four young college girls dad and I found dead in their car, mutilated, raped and killed. I asked him, hey did you ever have any as tight as those college girls before? I bet not. He made it clear he had been one of the rapists until he realized he had been tricked. These people are involved in a mass killing frenzy that includes degradation, rape, mutilation, every form of nastiness the two of you can imagine. They are educating their youngest, like the boy I told you about, to be just like them. These young kids are going along with that program all too willingly."

Dad said nothing. He looked at mom, squarely at her in the eyes, just nodded his head in agreement with me. Ruthie was crying. I remembered the old movie "RED DAWN" where the boys saw their parents being executed by invaders. I remembered where one of the boys told another to let his tears turn to hate. I mentioned the movie to Ruthie and mom.

I said "I don't want to hate these people. I would rather turn tail and run than kill them all. But if we start running they will pursue, and the probability is there are more of them of different groups toward the coast. So if it is up to me I want to stay and fight for as long as it is necessary to eliminate this group of murderers and rapists. Then maybe we can move on and do so at least without a pursuing militia of killers."

No one disagreed with that any further. Mom said, "Well, now we have that settled, let's entertain ourselves a little each night, play some cards, go down into the cave below where we can maybe play some music, dance a little, do something different than just fight and kill every night. Can we? Also you men need to teach us all about how to move in the forest, how to be quiet and invisible. If something happens to both of you we will try to get out of here and get back down toward Idaho Falls. Maybe if we travel in the daylight and if we are armed well enough we can make it to there safely. And the last thing is guys you need to teach us to shoot, no, not just to shoot but to shoot well so that we don't miss."

"Dad has pellet guns, doesn't he, mom?"

Dad nodded his head and mom said "Sure. I can shoot with those, okay. But I want to know how it feels to shoot a military weapon also." Ruthie chimed in at that point and said she too wanted to learn how to shoot the rifles and pistols we had been gathering. The house was full of them in fact. But none of them were loaded, ready to fire. We would not take the chance around the boys until we knew they were trustworthy with the idea of guns laying around loaded.

Instead of going on killing missions for the next few nights we worked with Ruthie and mom. We knew the area around the house was relatively safe. We knew we could travel into the woods for at least half a mile or so and not have to fear the militiamen. I think by that time they were as afraid of us as we were of them. I wanted to keep going back and killing more of them but dad thought we should take a break and work with the women.

We taught them to slide their feet just above the ground, and if they met any obstacle while doing so, move away from the obstacle, move a different direction. Ruthie got good at silent walking right away. Mom had a bit more of a struggle with it but she was learning. We taught them to move from tree to tree, slowly, watching, seeing all the critters of the forest as well as any humans that might be there. One night Ruthie and I went a little too far. We found ourselves in the outer edges of a search grid. I could tell by the way the guys in the grid were moving they were working that part of the forest in a way to try and discover any hiding places.

We waited. We moved away very slowly. When we got Ruthie to a safe spot I decided to take the nearest one to me down. It was easy even though he was wearing night vision. He was clumsy, loud, couldn't get out of his own way. I killed him with my knife, took his weapons and we left. When we were returning to the house I found Ruthie crying. I asked her what was wrong. All she could say was "I had put out of my mind what you and dad were having to do out there."

When we got back to the house Dad and I geared up and went back. We could not leave the body there. That would be an open invitation to search further in the area or the same direction. The others in the group had decided to make a camp for the night. We could hear them from a long way off. We could see their fire from a long way off. They never saw us. The sentry they posted was half asleep when dad cut his throat.

The other six of them, gathered around the fire with their weapons laid on the ground in front of them, died one by one with a bullet in his head. Two of them actually got their hands on their weapons before they died. We couldn't lug all of them to the canyon so we tied their legs together and drug them back the way they came. They had come from the roadblock.

We were making lots of noise as we came toward the roadblock. They had not posted any other sentries as before. There were four of them again. We shot them, stacked all the bodies in the back of the pick-ups and lit all of them afire.

We took everything from them we could carry, but ten rifles were too many. So we booby trapped several rifles of the older variety AR-15 and left them there. We were home well before dawn. As we were walking back it started raining. We thought that was a good thing. It would help obscure the drag marks. The others would find the locale where their buddies died eventually but by the time they did it would tell them little. The rain would make sure the tracks were gone.

When we got home I said to dad "Those silencers on the MP-5s are breaking down. Either we will have to use the pistols for a time or our knives more often. Or maybe we can fix the silencers. What do you think dad?"

"Nah. Once they go they cannot be fixed. We might as well take them off the guns now for all they are worth. And the nines, the pistols, will go the same way. I can try to add some materials into the silencers on the pistols but I don't think those on the MP-5's can be altered."

I left him to that task and went looking around in the cave. I found what I was looking for right away. It was a crossbow. Dad had several of them as I had recalled. I wondered if I still could shoot it. He came in while I was looking at it, trying to remember everything quirky about it and not doing that very well. He said "It still works and it is a very silent weapon if you hit in the head. But that can only happen from a very close distance, Will."

"Well if we go out tonight I think I will carry one and see what it can do if I can get close enough to one of those guys."

"You can bet they will be back out looking again, Will. They have decided this area must be where we are located. I am sure they will continue. The only question I have is how many of those fools can be left. Hell we must have killed at least thirty of them. If that kid was right, the one we talked to, there cannot be more than ten or so of the original group left."

"Some of that recent group we put into the pick-up tuck and burned, dad, were dressed in regular army fatigues, not camo but just army clothing. I wonder if they recruited some of the National Guard people. And there were a couple of those guys who had night vision. One of them you took care of had night vision. Of course he was an idiot too."

"Well if they are National Guardsmen they are incompetent ass-holes," my dad said. "What kind of a soldier would let an old man like me come up behind him with a knife standing in a clearing watching the area with night vision glasses?"

"I would say they just don't have much training or leadership, dad. And in a perverse kind of way it is a really good thing for us. Okay. It's getting late so let's get geared up. I am going to take the bow with us tonight as well as the silenced pistols and MP-5's as usual. One more thing. What do you think about taking one of their trucks, after we are done with them, driving it close enough to town to get in the woods and skirt around town and then head back here after we do a little recon work?"

"Sounds good to me but let's see how alert they are after losing those people in the rainy night a couple of nights ago. I think we had better begin to try and find out if any of the people in town are antagonistic to this militia group as well. We might want to conduct a raid on the police station to see if they are holding any townies as prisoners. We already know they are killing all the out of town people who come this way."

"Yeah. We need to begin to get enough information to know our enemy a little better, and the only place we can get the information is in town. So let's see what comes up tonight and whether we can get a little closer before heading back here."

We knew the militia had an idea of the route we had been taking to the roadblock area. We could tell they did by the sentries they posted in the forest. We killed them all out of necessity in order to deal with those in the roadblock. Again we thought it might be good to question one of them and we chose one of the sentries this time. There were many of them. Dad took the first. Another heard dad and came toward the first guy, yelling his name. I took him with the bow, shot him through the forehead. He dropped instantly and quietly. There were others. We could hear them easily. We took each of them out, one by one. All totaled we took out ten sentries in the night and four blockade guards. We did the same thing with the bodies we had done before.

Before we took out the last of the sentries he was scared half to death, firing rounds all over the place, yelling into the radio. Nothing happened. The helicopter pilot must not have been available. No one came screaming out of the town to "deal" with us. I knocked the guy out. I propped him up against a tree and trussed him up for the moment while dad took some of the dead toward the trucks. Dad would kill the guards on the road block by himself tonight. I was tasked with the prisoner.

"What is your name?"

"I am Staff Sergeant James Miller, my number is..." I interrupted him with a slap across his mouth.

"What army do you serve in Mr. Miller?"

"The Army of northwestern Montana, sir."

"There is no such army boy. You are just a bunch of murdering rapists who cannot handle real military people."

"Yes, sir, you are certainly right about not being able to handle you. How many people do you have," he asked.

"That was my next question to you Mr. Miller. How many people do you have in your army?"

"We have over a hundred now. There are some of us up the road in Arlee and St. Ignatius and some in Superior as well. We are growing every day. You should join us."

"How many people do you have right here in Frenchtown, Mr. Miller?"

"I'm not sure, sir. All I know is there are a lot of us in the police station and the State Police barracks."

"Are you holding any prisoners in Frenchtown, in the jail, Mr. Miller?"

"Oh, yes sir. We have quite a few actually. There are a couple of guys who used to be State Police. They are still there. I think the former Mayor is there along with his wife and children, and there are several teachers and lawyers there as well."

"Mr. Miller you have been very helpful. For that you get to live at least until another moment. Get up," I said, "we are going down to the roadblock."

"We have people down there, sir."

"No, you don't have people down there any longer Mr. Miller." I whistled so my dad would know we were coming and went on down to the pick-up trucks which were now filled with bodies and covered in gasoline out of the tank from each vehicle. "All right Mr. Miller, get inside the first truck and put your hands on top of the wheel. Are you carrying any kind of a knife?"

"Yes." He started to reach for it and I sapped him. He fell across the seat, unconscious. I pulled him up, tied him to the wheel and put his little Buck knife in his left hand. I waited until he was half awake, whistled and went back into the woods. Miller was free faster than the other boy and died in the same way when he tried to start the truck. The truck lit fire as a result of the explosion.

It took about ten minutes for two more trucks with six men in them came racing down the highway toward the fire. We had them in a cross fire. We killed them all before they ever stopped their trucks. Each of those trucks kept rolling on across the road to the freeway. We saw two more coming and did the same thing in the same way, this time using their SAW weapons that we had taken that night and one RPG. All in all we killed over twenty-five of them in one evening. Then we melted back into the forest and found our way home.

Ruthie asked no questions after I had cleaned up and came to bed. She held me tightly and we made love silently, but very passionately. I think probably my mother and father did the same thing. I know she loves him and I know he worships her. They are both attractive people who very easily could still be sexually active in their late fifties or early sixties, and well beyond. All Ruthie said to me throughout the night was "I love you my darling."

Chapter 5

Frenchtown, The War Continues

Once we had made the break from Guerilla warfare and taken a bunch of them down at once we had them on the defensive. We owned the night. They were afraid to sortie at night any longer. It was too dangerous for them. They thought their numbers increasing in their searches would insure them some level of safety. They thought more and more military equipment would give them an edge, a moment where they might be able to see us.

In Vietnam and Afghanistan we learned that the enemy owned the land at night and we owned it by day. It was what the circumstance had boiled down to in the area around our home and in Frenchtown itself as far as we could tell. But we needed to know more of who they were. We needed to know what they were planning if we could steal some of that information. We needed to know who was on their side, if anyone, from the town. So we packed food and ammunition carefully. We took a SAW each in case we got involved in a really serious firefight, and an RPG each to give us some artillery as well as the usual MP-5 and the silenced Beretta pistols.

We packed some dehydrated fruit, some small cans of chicken and a couple of MRE's each. We took a couple of small canteens each and water purification pills for when we would have to drink water from the streams in the area. We were armed for bear, packed as much weight as we could, and set off into the night via a route dad told me would shorten the distance to the town perimeter by about two or three miles from the trip I had taken earlier.

God, it had only been three weeks since I arrived. It seemed like we had been at war forever. We moved with extreme care and moved slowly. We figured if it took us two days to get in and two days to get out it would be fine. We were prepared to stay longer given the right set of circumstances but we didn't want to be in the open spaces of the town itself for long. As always we carried a small amount of Semtex, an all purpose plastic explosive that is easy to use and always gives good results.

Now and again as a person moves through the forest, if you do it slowly and alertly you will run onto animals. We saw a doe and its newborn fawn bedded down in a small copse of trees. She didn't bother about us because we seemed to be part of the natural surroundings. We did see a bear and he took off the opposite direction which was fine except that spooked animals are often a key to finding someone in the forest. We left the area he had been in with some additional haste but not movement which would be noticed as hasty.

As we came closer to town we began to smell the smoke of campfires. The first of those was a two man outpost with a radio. The radio was turned off. They were asleep in their bags. We dispatched them silently with our knives, left them rolled up in their bags, hid their weapons quite a ways off from where they were laying dead and went on. We decided to branch out right and left for an hour and then return to the spot we were in. I found two more sleeping sentry posts, dispatched the men in them and then went back. Dad had done pretty much the same. We whispered quietly. He said "They seem to have a perimeter set about two hundred yards into the forest. I would guess based on the guys we have taken out already there must be at least four or five more campsites like this. I think we should do them and then see if they have an inner perimeter." In about two hours that was done and we were back together again. We had each done five more camps. Time to move a little closer.

We crawled the last two hundred or so yards to the perimeter road of the town. There were trucks patrolling. There were three of them and each truck had two men in it. They seemed to be communicating with each other since we could see them using the radios as they drove by us. We took the first one and parked it next to a house which was totally darkened and in which the windows had been boarded up. The second one came along, stopped and pulled over to see what the other two guys were doing when we took them. The third was just driving along, listening to music. We pulled that truck in beside the others, dumped the six bodies in the bed of one of the trucks, booby trapped one of them and then donning one of their hats and keeping it down low drove the entire perimeter of the town.

There was an area in the middle of town that was highly illuminated. They had put up fenced areas for keeping locals by day and had them well lighted at night. Those were around the State Patrol Office. Dad had mentioned the patrol office had a larger jail than the town facility so they were likely to be keeping prisoners in the State Patrol Office. We watched for a while and saw that there were only a few guards. Everyone else seemed to be asleep. One came out to take a leak. He was pinned to a tree by the arrow from the crossbow that went through his head.

Someone came out to look for him. That guy made the mistake of stepping into the shadows and taking a nine millimeter bullet from my dad's pistol through his head. A third guy stood in the door of the jail and yelled for his buddies. That gave us the clue that he was the last of them. I took him inside very quickly with a knife in my hands and at his throat. I asked who was being detained there. He told me. I had him take me to the mayor and the two State Police Officers. We got them out of their cells, took them outside and asked if they were willing to try for Missoula or maybe even further south depending on what was going on in Missoula. They all agreed and we armed them and took them back to the trucks after creating a Semtex event that would happen within half an hour. The mayor took one truck and left. The Statie's took another truck and left vowing to kill those at the roadblock on Hwy.93. I told them of the raping and murdering these militia people had been doing. They left determined to do damage to those on the roadblock we had attacked repeatedly.

One thing the Sgt. of State Police did say before leaving was, "They think you guys are an army of thousands and they are scared shitless. They want to negotiate with someone but they put out people in an attempt to do that and their people disappear or show up dead. You guys are doing great work." The one thing we asked him to do if it were possible was to get us a couple of people who were Seals, Marine Recon, the like, to reinforce our battle group. They said they would try. We told the Statie's we would look for them once a week in the area of the dead Jeep that was still sitting on Hwy. 93, the one we took out.

We took the truck we had left, full of dead bodies, and drove north toward Arlee to see if there was a roadblock there. Four guys manned it in two trucks. Only two of them were visible and we found out the other two were in their sleeping bags in the beds of the trucks sound asleep. When we pulled up to the stop area one of each of the guys came to the door on each side of the truck. Dad shot one of them and I shot the other. We talked to one of the sleepers for a little while and then set his truck up for him to take it home. It was getting on toward 4:30 a.m. by that time.

We left them there, heard the truck explode, drove the truck we were in back to the town perimeter and went back into the forest. We only had two hours in which to find a place and hide out. It was not hard. We were asleep most of the day while we listened occasionally to the helicopter or other men running through the woods as fast as they could to avoid traps and trying to avoid getting killed by some boogeyman.

Near to 7:30 a.m. we heard a loud explosion reverberate through the trees. We knew what that was. It was the State Police building. When we emptied the night before we booby trapped it with a large amount of the Semtex we were carrying. There would not be much left of that place we thought. It narrowed the militiamen's possibilities for incarcerating people. That might mean they would allow townspeople to live in their homes. That would eventually be good for us. We had to marshal some support amongst the townspeople, at least over time, to keep up this barrage. We were largely self contained but in time we would need to be in town and have places of refuge there.

On this sortie we had marked in our memories several homes which appeared to be unoccupied and boarded up. They would be suitable for a momentary rest stop. But we had to be able to trust our enemies would not find our places of refuge easily. If we could depend on some of the locals to hide us out it would be a lot less daunting.

When we got back deep into the forest this time we heard a flurry of activity coming along the trails. There were many ATV's being used this time instead of the pick-up trucks. There were a few pick-ups to be sure but many more ATV's. We went to ground in a natural cave that we had discovered in our travels.

It was shallow, probably had been a refuge for a bear in the past, and might well be the same again in time as our scent wore off. It was in a heavily shadowed area of the forest. It was in an area where there was much undergrowth and it would be ripe for a forest fire if one got started in that area. Dad and I worried some about the idea of a forest fire.

With all the gunfire that was coming from the people searching, misdirected gunfire, shooting just to be shooting, we hoped no tracer rounds were going out of those guns that might set a fire. The forest was our friend, our ally, our place to be free to move and sally toward the town. Without the forest we would have been spotted very easily and probably have been dead meat a long time ago.

We watched from our hidey hole as two ATV's came by our place several times. They never stopped, never looked in our direction, and never paid any heed to who might be hiding in the area. This was all a matter of form to them. They had been attacked and they assumed the attack came from the forest. So they set out to make whoever was assailing them know it was not safe to do so. The same two ATV's came by again. We had timed them the first two times they came by.

We had about thirty minutes before they came back. It was full daylight and yet in that area it was dark enough so that visibility was at least impaired to a small degree. We set up wires across the area where each of the ATV's would cross which would hit the riders, two to an ATV, straight across the faces. The wires worked perfectly.

The ATV's were knocked down and the kill switch that each driver was wearing worked perfectly. It was still noisy in that area, but not nearby. We dispatched the riders, took their equipment, and hid their bodies in leaves and branches in a small depression near the trail. We took the ATV's and hid them back in the trees with branches covering them. They could be seen but only from a very short distance. We went back to our copse. Soon it would be dark and we would head home as the militiamen gave up the forest and ran for cover.

Both dad and I were tiring of the killing. It was not what we would have preferred to be doing. But we saw no other way to deal with these bastards. Every time we went to the roadblock we found at least two or three carloads of dead bodies, poor travelers trying their damndest to get home or close to home or friends. We kept telling each other war is hell. It was the label, that of war, which made this so strange. How could we call this war? It was our own people?

No, it was not our own people. These people were some kind of aberration. They were some devil's seed as far as we could tell. The several of them we had interrogated were fearful of death but proud as hell of their accomplishments as killers and rapists. I will never forget the look on the face of the young boy who when I asked him about getting some of that tight stuff was simply evil looking in his satisfaction and the remembrance of his conquest. What other term could we use but war? No matter, if they caught us they would kill us all, rape and murder our wives, murder my sons. We would not see it happen, not as long as we could fight, could take them out two or three or ten at a time. Attrition would eventually take care of the bastards, I thought. And who knows, maybe in time the Statie's we let go would get us some reinforcements in here. We would check on the possibility every other night from now on if it were possible.

Both dad and I had been neglecting our brides and the children. We took them all down into the cave where the acoustics were naturally shut down and let them all plink with twenty-two caliber rifles and pistols. Then after shooting the smaller twenty-two shells for a while we let them cap off a clip each of the .223 rounds that fired from the AR-15's, the M-16's and the SAW weapons. Those were louder and produced more recoil. They surprised my wife quite a bit and scared my sons a little. It was okay with me for the present. The boys needed to begin to learn but they were sure as the world too young to have to aim a rifle at a man and shoot.

My mom and my wife were not the kind of people who could do the work dad and I had been tending to but they would be able, in a dire situation, to use a weapon. We were just making sure they could do it without flinching from the noise or the recoil. By then we had enough .223 ammunition that we had confiscated from the militiamen to start another war in the next county.

After practice that afternoon we listened to RUSA again for a while and tried the television but got nothing. We had heard no more about the "invasion" of our country for over a week. We were all a bit anxious about that. We rested until around 7:30 that evening, ate a few bites of some delicious baked chicken that my mother and Ruthie prepared for us from canned foods combined with MRE's and geared up.

We were both carrying crossbows all the time now. Dad had been practicing with his and if anything was a better shooter with that tool than I was. We left the house and headed toward Charley and Berne-ice's place where we could be close to the highway without being seen, to await the possible arrival of any new troops. None came.

On the way to the potential rendezvous site we had seen and dis-patched another six of the sentries that the militia was putting out into the forest each night. We dragged them out of the forest after we waited for any newcomers and took them to the other side of the road past Charley's house to throw into a depressed area. It took a little while to do it but the bodies were taken away from the sites where they had died.

We had to dodge a patrol which was going up and down highway 93 consisting of a bunch of variously dressed idiots in a Humvee that had a top mounted machine gun. I had been coveting a machine gun, light weight .223 variety that of our military was using now, for quite a while. There were, as it turned out, five men in the unit. As the RPG we had begun to carry with us on a regular basis entered the driver's door I could see there was no armor. The RPG was fired from such a short range no one even cried out. The four inside the Humvee were killed instantly while the top gunner had his legs cut nearly off by the explosion. We sent him on his way by being at the vehicle within five seconds of the explosion occurring. I dismounted the belt fed gun and took it with me.

It turned out to be a thirty caliber weapon, 7.62 millimeter is the NATO designation I believe, and therefore was a little heavier but it was in good shape. There was an extra canister of ammunition in the Humvee. Dad took that and we left the area. No one was coming in the night except for more militiamen and then only as a body recovery detail. They were pulling back out of the woods at night more and more. As the song says which used to be sung about Vietnam all the time, "Another one bites the dust." Only in this case it was ten more. Damn, where the hell were all their men coming from?

We knew the military base up the road near Arlee was virtually gone now. We had seen a Humvee, a larger truck and a lot of camo painted ATV's already. But the militia was still using its favorite transportation, the pick-up truck for the most part. We had seen the helicopter change and become equipped with military weapons, particularly machine guns. We assumed those were mounted by members of the National Guard since it was unlikely that the militiamen would have known how to do that.

The militia had machine guns that had to have come from the base as well as SAW's and M-4 rifles with selector switches for burst, single or full automatic fire. We could not know how much of the armory was already in our hands. There was a lot. But the percentage of weapons taken by the militia? Impossible to know unless we went to Arlee and found some records of what had been there before the war started. But we could look at the population figures for Frenchtown if the internet was still operating.

We had dad's wi-fi setup dialed up the next morning, trying to find out what population figures existed for Frenchtown. We got into Wikipedia without too much ado which was very surprising to us. The estimates of population were a little over 2500 people of which about 55% were male and of that group about 35% were less than forty years of age. We had not seen any large, fat men, banker types, lawyer types, in the trees. All the men we had encountered were under 40 years of age or at most in that range. We estimated the number of men potentially available in Frenchtown at the outset of the nuclear war would have been about one thousand, three hundred and seventy-five and that was all of the men that were there. The population which had existed which was less than forty years of age was about eight hundred and seventy five people.

The total we came up with included such men as the Statie's we had let go, the town policemen which we assumed were dead, the mayor and a few of his friends, again we had let him go with the Statie's. As near as we could tell by then we were averaging about ten to fifteen of them a night. Some nights there had been more, some less. But the number that we had eliminated had started to swell drastically. We had taken care of well over a hundred of those people. If we made the assumption that some of the town's men refused to serve in this army of northwestern Montana we felt it was possible we had eliminated at least a fourth of their strength. Knowing those things we also knew that it had to continue for a time.

Chapter 6

Eileen Powers

Mom said to Dad the next morning when all of us were having a brunch together "Gene, do you remember the lady who ran the library? I think her name was Eileen Powers."

"Sure. She was always very pleasant to deal with, courteous to you and I both in every way. And she helped us with setting up our projects out here a couple of times."

Mom looked at him and in a low tone of voice said "I wonder if she is still alive."

Dad probably was thinking about exactly the thoughts mom was having. He said, "Oh crap, she would know exactly where we are, wouldn't she?" Mom nodded her head. Dad said "Didn't she come out here two or three times when we were working on the place?"

"Yes, honey, yes she did. She and I talked a lot about the kind of plants I could grow in artificial light and whether we could find a way to have a garden with things like tomatoes, turnips, melons. Crap, she even knows a lot about the cave I'm afraid. She and I spent a lot of time down there exploring and trying to figure out whether the salinity in the cave would damage plants or assist their growth."

"Do you remember exactly where she lived in town?"

"Yes. She was about two streets in from the outside circle and was about three houses to the south of the library itself."

"Didn't she have a son?"

"Yes," mom said, "and as I recall he was a bit of a ne'er do well. He would be a natural for the kinds of things you two have told us were happening to the outsiders coming through the area. Oh God, honey, if she talked to him about us it would be because he was in the militia movement and she figured out it was probably you knocking them down so badly."

"Well I guess we have a mission for tonight, Will. We have got to see to it somehow that she gets the hell out of here and that her son is eliminated without her knowing it was done by us. God this is a ticklish one."

We both knew unfortunately the death of Eileen Powers might have to rest on our consciences. Certainly her son was one of our most likely candidates to be a militia man if we could find him. What a quandary to be in. A nice woman, a woman with class and a sense of courtesy which was remarkable, a woman with a son whose likely membership in the militia could not be refuted. Would both have to die? God how I hoped the horror of war would not have to be visited on our home. But of course the issue lay heavy in the air that Eileen Powers had information about us no one else possessed, no one else could have if we were to continue to survive and fight the war.

Dad and I went to bed in the late morning and slept into the middle of the afternoon. We spent the rest of the afternoon thinking carefully about everything involved in the situation with Eileen Powers. But she was not a murderer. Or was she? Was she a militia person? Was her son a militia person? Had he attempted to query her about whether she might know someone capable of doing what we were doing if he was militia? There were too many unanswered questions. We had to find the answers to some of them at least. Then we could take whatever action was necessary to bring this potential threat to an end.

Sleep was difficult. My kids were loud. My mind was churning. My heart was heavy for my mom. Finally I slept and then in what seemed no time at all, dad awakened me. Around eight p.m. we geared up, said our goodbyes to our wives and kids, and took off toward town. We were mentally in a bit of a hurry, but physically we were careful as usual.

It was imperative to be careful and it was for a necessary purpose as we soon learned. The ring of sentries was further into the forest this time. This time there were three sentries in each camp. We went first to the camp furthest away to the north. It was neutralized in seconds. These sentries acted like they were drugged they were so passive. One went down with an arrow. One went down with a pistol shot. The third went down with a second arrow. He did not try to shoot. He did not try to run away. He died.

The next camp found all three militiamen asleep and a few minutes later they were permanently so. We worked our way across the camps which were set within minutes of each other, taking our time, watching for booby traps or mine placements. We did find one set of Claymore mines placed toward our house which could have been destructive to us had we come from the right direction. But we didn't. We came from behind them and they never knew we were there. We saw the cords going to the Claymores, disabled them, stowed them and the prima cord in our packs and went on to the next group.

We finished with the sentries, ten sets of three, at about one o'clock in the morning. None survived, none made warnings to any of the others or to the central command of the militia units. We went on toward town then and seeing nothing of any threat went into the town itself. We saw some new searchlight and high intensity lamp placements but they were not in areas that threatened us yet. We moved through the first couple of streets, found the library and found Eileen's home. It was boarded up.

We went back to the library which was too highly illuminated for us to chance entry. We saw a woman working at a desk in the library. According to dad, it was Eileen. We saw her turn off the lights, close the door and walk away from the building. We watched, waited and then saw there were two guys moving with her but behind the cover of darkness around several nearby homes. I took one of them with the bow as he came close to me. Dad took the other with his pistol. Eileen heard us and scurried toward me in an attempt to get away from the circumstances.

I stopped Eileen and shushed her. She was obviously scared half to death of the way I looked. I held her quietly and told her she would not be harmed, and that dad wanted to talk with her. Dad got there in a minute or so. She recognized his voice when he said "Eileen, are you all right?"

"Oh Gene, it is you," she said. "I thought it might be you. They tried to get it out of me who it might be but I kept telling them that I had no idea. They only talked to me once. But I think they still suspect I know who it is they are fighting. What can I do, Gene?"

"Come with us, Eileen. We cannot help your son. He is part of this is he not?"

"Yes, yes I am afraid he is one of the leaders of the group. He probably has more education than the rest of them put together and he is one of the leaders."

"Will you come with us, Eileen?"

"Can I change clothes?"

"No, it is a trek to take and we will be lucky to finish before dawn so it is best we go now."

"Will I stay with you all the time until this thing is over, Gene?"

"We will talk about the possibilities, Eileen. We have released some State Police Officers who are going to try and help us. We may try to get you out of here by asking their help. We will have to wait and see. One question, Eileen. Have you seen your son looking through your stuff lately?"

"Several times in fact, Gene. Why do you ask?"

He is a sly old dog. The thought had come to him about the same time as I thought of the potential for a tracking device. What kind of shoes are you wearing, Eileen?" dad asked.

"Why, I am wearing the only ones they left me, my tennis shoes."

"Would you take off the left one for me now please, Eileen?" She did. He found a tracking device in a cut out spot in the area of the heel. When he asked about it she said she thought they had been repaired. There was another in the other shoe. We disposed of both. We searched her purse and found two more. Finally we asked her to look in her bra and her belt to see if there were any others. There were. She was a walking roadmap to wherever. We also asked if she had received any injections since the start of the militia activities. She responded negatively to our question.

We finally felt we could go on into the forest and did so. We knew there were no sentries left to face so we made haste on the animal trail for a while and then skirted it and went into the forest itself. She was surprised when we taught her how to use the night vision devices we had taken from some of the dead sentries at how well she could see without a light of any kind.

We arrived back at the house much earlier than usual. It was nearing four a.m. We woke mom up and Ruthie awakened as well. They went into the kitchen and made coffee and chattered as three women will do. We went into the kitchen, had some coffee with them and all of us then went to bed. It seemed we had not had to do the ultimate kind of dirty act war so often demands. We were both satisfied with not having to kill her. We also were unaware we had killed her son in the sentry circle.

As we walked into the kitchen, Eileen said to both of us, "My, you two have surely wreaked havoc in the militia in the last three weeks or so. My son told me they have lost over a hundred men. My goodness did you do all that by yourselves?"

"Before we talk about the deaths, Eileen, I have to ask you how you feel about this whole Army of northwestern Montana or whatever they are calling themselves now."

"Well they have provided some security for all of us in the town. I mean we have heard there is a shooting war on in the southern U.S. between the U.S. Army and the Cubans. The Cubans invaded Florida almost immediately after the nuclear war was over. Or at least it seems like it is over."

"So what do you think the overall impression of the militia would be in the town, Eileen?"

"I think it's mostly favorable. They have been able to keep everyone who needs it from paying exorbitant amounts of money for gasoline. Actually I saw a gasoline truck in town last week. It was colored in the army green but I thought it was probably part of the militia thing. And there are no major food shortages yet."

"The banks opened their doors a couple of weeks after the events of the nuclear exchange. They gave us all $ 5,000.00 as a starter fund for us to use for food and gasoline, those sorts of necessities. They promised they would do that every month or if we needed extra money at any point in time all we have to do is ask. When we have electric power it is from large gasoline driven generators that come from the army also. The militia uses those at night to see to it there is no crime in the town. It is a security thing I guess. So all in all I guess they have been doing a pretty good job. And I expect my take is how most of the people in town would see it. I don't think you folks should count on any help from anyone there."

"Thank you for your candor, Eileen. How do you feel toward us personally?"

"Well, I love Mrs. de Young, you know I love you my dear, and I have always thought well of Mr. de Young. I think maybe you ought to try and talk to the leaders of the militia and see if you can't work something out."

"Have you seen any cars around town with license plates from Nebraska, Oklahoma, states other than those which are not from Montana, Eileen?"

"Yes, I have seen some of those. I supposed they were on their way toward the coast. The coast seems relatively safe for everyone."

"You had better get hold of yourself, Eileen. We have a lot to tell you about your militia group," said dad. "I am going to have Will here start."

"I headed up here when I knew there was a really good chance we were going to have a nuclear war, Eileen. I know we have not met before but I hope you won't mind my using your first name."

She nodded. I continued. "The day I arrived in Missoula I had been warned some militia people had been doing some strange stuff up in this area. I stopped on my way up Hwy. 93 and pulled into a home site there just about a mile before the turn off for Frenchtown. It turned out my parents knew the people who lived there very well, Eileen. You might have known Charley and Berneice also. Apparently they were quite popular in the area."

She nodded. I continued. "I found them dead in their dining room. They had been tortured quite evidently. She had been raped and probably repeatedly. They were shot to death after all these things occurred." She began to cry.

Mom patted her on the shoulder, gave her some tissue to wipe her eyes and I continued. "The deaths of Charley and Berneice are far from the worst of it, Eileen. That first night I found some things in Charley's place that enabled me to walk through the forest toward Frenchtown. As I came to the edge of town there was a roadblock on the highway. I watched while four men raped a young woman. Her husband had been shot dead on the street. I could do nothing then except go on toward town unless I shot and killed the woman. But I had no idea of what was going on. So I walked further. I was shot at just as dusk fell and some began to chase me. I was able to get away and after two days of being chased by a series of pick-up trucks, hearing the men talking about torturing me to find out what I had seen, and having to kill two men I made it home."

"Oh my God," Eileen said, sobbing, "I was so afraid those sorts of things were being done. Do you know where the money came from, Will?"

"Of course it came from hundreds of travelers who were headed north or to the coast who have been killed by the militia. That came along with their gasoline, their cars, children, young people. I saw one car with four dead girls in it who could not have been more than seventeen or eighteen years old each. They were naked, cut up, dead, raped, disfigured and killed. Sure the money, everything came from the people those militiamen are killing at the roadblocks."

"Oh God can you get me out of here, out of this area?"

"Well, we can try, Eileen. We will see what we can do as soon as it is possible," dad said. "But for now you will have to stay here. Oh, and I have to warn you there are booby traps all over the area. If you do not know where they are they would probably cause you to be hurt very badly or could even kill you. So trying to get out of here and going back to town is not a good idea."

She put her hand to her face, looked at dad and asked, "Oh, Gene, you are not threatening me are you? Threats are so beneath you."

"Eileen, I am not threatening you. I am telling you we had a choice to make when we went to town tonight. The choice was to bring you back or kill you. We brought you back in hopes we might get you out of the area and have you tell our story to the authorities we hope still exist in Missoula or elsewhere. No, Eileen. I am not threatening you. I want you to live to be able to give the authorities the information we have given to you. It might not result in anything at all but maybe, just maybe there is someone who can marshal enough forces against these militia idiots so we can stop having to kill them one by one. If we didn't have to kill them it would be good, wouldn't it?"

She agreed. We asked mom to take her to the bathroom, give her a shower and check her clothes for any more tracking devices. Mom came out in a few minutes and shook her head. We decided, since there was still a couple of hours of dark left, to take a look at what was going on around our "compound." I set the machine gun up in one of the spider holes. We had a total of ten spider holes.

We had SAW weapons in four of those, a machine gun in one other and the MP-5's that could be used in two others. And in addition to those weapons we had many M-4's with selector switches that we could fire full automatic if we wanted. The tunnels running from one spider hole to another would, if necessary, give us one hellatious advantage over anyone coming toward our home. We had ammunition stored in each of them in copious amounts we had confiscated from the militiamen we had killed. We checked each of those spider holes and made sure ammunition and weapons were at the ready. Then we went out and checked various devices which would discourage anyone from coming there. Dad had them put up through the years. Among those were Claymore mines which he had mounted in the crotch of several trees with full field of fire across the most obvious avenues of approach to the house. It seemed like everything was quiet, all was as it should be and we went back in and went to sleep.

Through the next day, in the time when the militia owned the hours, we could see and hear helicopters, now more than one, and trucks and ATV's running all over the forest. They were making their own trails, tearing the floor of the forest to pieces, probably insuring that the next rainfall of any substance would create some flooding somewhere.

It was all sound and fury with nothing accomplished though. So we waited for our time, for the night. It was one of the nights that we were supposed to be at the rendezvous point to meet the State Police near to 8:00 p.m. so we left the house early. We left Eileen with mom, Ruthie and the kids.

When we were getting close to the rendezvous point we started to see some movement in the trees along the right of way to the highway.

It was clear that these were not typical militia people but we could not identify them yet. I had the radio we had exchanged with the State Police on the appropriate channel and an ear bud in so no sound would come out of the radio. Over the radio I heard "Where the hell are you guys?"

My answer was a simple one. "Fi," I said. The password we had worked out with the State people was Semper Fi in return. "What the hell are you doing," was what I got in return. I had been moving closer to the guy who was talking all the time. I saw him standing next to a tree, three guys around him. He was badly cut up and it became evident to me that he was to be of help to us but had been spotted and caught by the militiamen. Dad and I exchanged looks and signs of our own. I waited. Dad was in position by my count of twenty. I killed the one on my end, he killed the one on his end and I killed the third one in that order. The first two went down by bow. The last by silenced pistol. We waited.

Our boy, the one who had been tortured, said "Semper Fi." We moved toward him very slowly and carefully. I saw one more that was hiding behind him, trying to peer out between our guy's legs and from behind a tree. He never saw or heard dad. I heard the sound of a throat being cut. Our guy sank to the ground. Dad walked around and looked at him. Our guy was dead. They had cut him up too badly, too many places and too many times. I heard a radio squelch on the radio he was holding. I spoke into it and said, "Fi. Semper Fi is no more." The squelch answered and a car took off toward Missoula.

While dad stripped the weapons and night vision gear off the four dead guys I checked for I.D. on the body of our dead colleague. I found none except that on his right wrist there was tattooed the insignia of a Seal. In one pocket of the guy that dad had snuck up on, we found the I.D. His name was Ken Stills. He was gone and we never got to talk with him at all. Ken had brought with him another set of night vision gear. That was evident by the number of items we found. There was another MP-5 as well with a large number of extra clips in his vest. And behind one of the clips in his vest I found a note. It would wait until we got home. I was pissed and wanted a little payback. One of ours for four of theirs was not enough. Dad said "Whatever you want to do, son."

We went toward the roadblock. We moved even more carefully now because of capture and death of Ken Stills. We found a series of sentry posts. They seemed more alert but the result of their being there was the same as those of their brethren who had gone before them. There were twelve more of them before the night was over. Since it was only a few hundred yards from where we found Ken to the roadblock we took his body there and put it into the fire we lit to burn the other sixteen that we had killed that night. The only thing other than the loss of Ken Still which was negative about the night was that the militiamen seemed to be getting some training from someone or somewhere.

When we got home we took the note out and I read it to the family. It said simply, "We will come every other night now. If we hear from you tonight and there is a problem we will go to the alternate location on the next trip. We hope to bring another man with us the next time. We will try to bring more and more reinforcements as time goes along. We have word out to the proper locations and people and we are assured that they will get you some help."

Eileen asked after I read the note, "Did they bring you some help tonight?" Dad, at whom she was looking and to whom she seemed to be directing the question, just nodded.

She asked, "Where is he, who is he, where are they coming from? What is going on?"

"He is dead," my father said. "His name was Ken Stills. I don't know where he came from, I only know he was an American sailor, a Navy Seal. Somehow they got onto the meeting place or they figured it out because we went there too often, I'm not sure what happened. Whatever it was Ken is dead along with a few others."

"Oh my God, Gene, you didn't kill my boy tonight, did you?"

"I don't think so unless he looks a lot different than he did the last time I saw him Eileen. But why would he have been there?"

She was crying again, and said "I overheard him talking to one of his men two days ago and telling the guy they thought they knew where we were meeting people from out of town. Was that close to the drive in to Charley's property?"

"Yes, Eileen, it was. But we will not be there the next time."

"But where can you go," she asked?

"Don't worry, Eileen. We already have another meeting place set up and we will all go there tomorrow night so you can get down to Missoula. From there you will be on your own. How much money did you have in your purse by the way?"

"The $5,000.00 they gave me at the bank."

"Okay. We have been gathering a lot of money from the militiamen so we will give you another $50,000.00 to take with you in case things are more expensive than they should be. The three of us will leave here tomorrow at dusk. You will have to learn to follow our lead, to be quiet and to say and do nothing at all when we tell you. Do you understand?"

"Yes. I know they will be looking for you. And I know they believe you are meeting other people down toward where Charley and Berneice lived. But I can be quiet."

"Even if we have to do some killing? And the likelihood of more killing is very strong, Eileen. Can you keep quiet then?"

"Oh my. It will be hard but I will have to, won't I."

"Unless you want the militiamen to shoot you down you will have to be quiet no matter what. They will not hesitate to kill you after the trackers were found and your tails were killed."

"What do you mean my tails were killed?"

"When you left the library night before last you had two men following you. Didn't you know?"

"No."

"They died. If we were going to get you out of there it had to take place."

"Oh my God, Will, I'm sorry you had to do that."

"Are you sorry for the girls who were raped, Eileen? Even if it was your son doing it?"

Dad stepped in at that point. He knew I was pissed. He also knew that if she tried to give us away she would die and I would not hesitate to kill her. I showed her how we walked in the forest. I told her she would be between dad and I and she would not know how far I was behind her so follow dad, do what he says to do and everything will work out fine. Mom was looking at me the entire time. At one point, standing behind Eileen, she shook her head and walked into the kitchen without saying anything.

When we were done, dad and I went to bed and got some sleep. We left later than usual. The secondary meeting place was set for an hour later in our original plans. We walked slowly, trying to teach Eileen along the way. But she was noisy and a slow learner, or she was being obstructive. I was not sure which. We were close to the meeting place, more than an hour early, so we called a halt for a drink of water and a rest and pit stop if needed.

Apparently, dad and I had been distracted by the noise Eileen was making. I don't know. Maybe we were just being careless that night. But I heard a noise which was out of place and knew we were going to be under attack. I whistled to dad lowly and we both prepared. There were three of them. They had night vision and they were better than any we had faced yet. I saw the first one from the flank in time to shoot him with the bow under the chin. The arrow came out the top of his head.

Eileen saw this, stood up and started puking. The second guy saw her and stuck her in the middle of the chest with what looked to be a bayonet. It got stuck. I shot him between the eyes. Then I saw that dad was down and the guy over top of him was going to kill him. I shot that guy in the side of the head. His head nearly exploded on the other side. It got quiet in a hurry, except for Eileen's moaning.

I took the bayonet out of her. I bandaged her chest wound though I had no hope she would survive. She didn't. Within a minute she was gone. Dad was with me when she left us. He had seen what happened to her, tried to turn and got knocked down by the butt of a rifle by the guy I killed.

Dad had a nasty gash on his forehead. I stanched the flow of his blood and covered it with one of the military camo bandages that came with our kits. I gave him a couple of anti-biotics and several Ibuprofen. He had to stay sharp until we got home. We wondered why there were not more people. We wondered if somehow Eileen had gotten word to them. We wondered if the stumbling around and noisiness was not for their benefit.

We left the area after policing the weapons and ammunition as well as some canned goods the guys were carrying. One of them was "tatted" and I took the time to look. The "tats" were from prison and he was an Aryan Brotherhood member. So we discovered where they were getting their new recruits. I guess the new one were in congruity with the kind of criminal behaviors the militia had been exhibiting before.

We went to the meeting place. We got there early and waited in really good hiding places. Three militiamen came along. We killed them. Three more came along a little while later. We killed them. Four more came along a little later. We killed them. We wondered if they were supposed to be setting up to meet our people. Four more came along. We killed three of them and took one prisoner.

I asked the prisoner if any more were coming. He said he didn't know. He was being a smart ass. I gagged him and cut off his trigger finger with my knife. He screamed for a minute. I asked him again if any more were coming. He said he didn't know. I gagged him again and cut off the second finger on his right hand. He screamed, I sapped him, he went out and I cut his throat. Asshole.

About fifteen minutes before rendezvous time four more came along. We shot all of them. We were stacking their bodies in a pickup truck. Our guys came and we left with one more in our group. His name was Jim Martinez. He was from Missoula, had grown up there, and had gone to school there, including University of Montana. He was the army equivalent of a Recon Marine I guess, that being a Green Beret, Special Forces type. We told him what we were going to do with the bodies. He said "No problem."

We drove the truck to a point about a hundred yards from the road-block, set the steering wheel with rope and put a rock on the acceler-ator, put it in gear and let it go and crash into the roadblock. All four of the men working the roadblock were standing there looking at the truck when we set off the Semtex that blew the hell out of all of them.

Not a bad night given everything except of course for Eileen. Twenty-five more of theirs gone and one of ours slightly wounded for the first time. We went back and retrieved Eileen's body, put a note on it asking for a Christian burial, took it to the perimeter of the town that I had first seen only three weeks earlier, rolled it onto the street and beat feet. We were home before midnight.

After the initial rounds of introductions between Jim, mom and Ruthie, and after dad's forehead was cleaned up and Mom treated it with anti-biotic cream and sewed it up, we sat down and told the women the entire story. It was sad to lose Eileen. She had given us good information and been a friend to mom and dad in the past, and seemed like a nice lady. I still wonder to the day I am writing this whether she knew exactly what she was doing making noise.

The appearance of the first three militiamen, everything taken to-gether, it is just a little too coincidental for me. I don't really believe much in coincidences in war. There was nothing more to be done about it. As we talked, mom asked us for a moment of silence. We all joined hands, prayed in our own way for her soul and then the moment we had in the life of Eileen Powers was over. We had no way of knowing her family had been decimated by the events in Frenchtown.

Chapter 7

Jim Martinez and Friends

"The two guys from the State Police said to say hello to you guys and tell you thanks again for getting them out of the jail. The militia had told the two of them they were going to be executed the next day. They are very grateful to you two. Believe me when I tell you that."

"It's nice to know we did some good for someone," Dad said. "Unfortunately, it didn't work out for Eileen Powers. She was the woman we left in town tonight. We were trying to get her to Missoula. We were going to send her back with the guys that brought you in."

"Jesus, Powers you said? She was one of the ringleaders of the whole deal Mr. de Young. Her son was like the third in command in the militia outfit and she was calling the shots right down the line. According to what the State Police guys told me she got the boys to go to the armory and get all the weapons they have, I guess I should say had, looking at this place. She was the one who started the killing off the passers through so the militia could gather as much money as it could get. They robbed a couple of banks as well. They got all the cash out of the local banks right away, hit the banks in Arlee and Alberton within the first week. Jesus guys, you were damned lucky she didn't lead them right to you."

Mom sat there looking at Jim for a minute and said, "Are you sure about all of this Mr. Martinez? The State Police guys told you this? And they heard all this stuff going on while they were in jail?"

"Yes ma'am. There is no doubt. She was the brains behind the whole operation."

"God, dad, we bought her line in every respect. Do you think she had some kind of implanted tracking device on her?"

"I doubt it son. She is dead now anyway. And her own people killed her. What an incredibly ironic turn of events! And to think we gave her $50,000.00 from the money we have confiscated from those assholes."

"It's all right, dad." I took the packet of money we had given her out of my pack and threw it on the table. "I cannot tell you why but I always had the oddest feeling about that woman, like she was playing all of us. That is why I wanted to take the rear tonight, dad. I wanted the control going with hanging back a little, getting the chance to see what is developing and then react to it. You taught me well in that regard Major."

"You two are both Recon, aren't you?" asked Jim.

"Yes, we both were in that part of the Marine Corps at one time or another in our brief or long careers," my father responded. "I always thought I learned more about life and about how to live in extreme circumstances in that training than I learned in any other setting in my lifetime. Do you agree with that, Will?"

"Yes, Dad, I do. And ever since arriving at Charley and Berneice's place last month I have been damned glad that we both had the training and could still use it to our benefit. Those people, Jim, have been trying to kill me and my family as well, for nearly a month now. My dad and I have whittled their numbers down a little, or so we thought until tonight. And our training is what has held us up, has made it possible for us to defeat those yokels every time in every way."

"Well, sir," Jim spoke to my dad, "and you too, Will," he continued, "we want to send in a lot of troops and take this town back, but we wanted to recon the place first. Can we do it safely?"

"No. And I don't think a pitched battle would ever occur if you sent a bunch of troops in here. What you would have then is a garrison against which these fools could chip away in Guerilla style warfare. And it would suit them a hell of a lot better than what they are doing now," my Dad responded.

Jim asked "What are they doing now?"

"They are a garrison fighting against a Guerilla force that is kicking their ass off every night. They own the day at this point. But we own the night. it has become increasingly more evident in the last week or so. And now their mastermind is dead I bet it gets easier yet to kill those bastards."

Jim was a little surprised and put out by our comments at that point. He said "You mean to tell me you have been going out night after night, conducting guerilla raids to kill a bunch of them off, to defeat them by attrition? How the hell could you do that? This is the United States of America."

"Obviously you have not been around an area where these bozos have been doing their thing before tonight, Jim. Did you not notice the cars parked beside the road at the roadblock when we attacked there," my dad asked?

"Yes sir, I saw them. But what do they mean?"

"You didn't go and take a look in any of them, did you Jim?"

"No, no I didn't, Will. Again, why is it important?"

"You tell him, Will," my dad said.

"I will make this brief, Jim. In those cars you would have found regular citizens of this United States of America. Every one of those average citizens would have been tortured and killed. All the women would have been raped and then mutilated. All the young girls would have been raped, no matter if they were teenagers or in their twenties. All the children, boys and girls alike, of an age less than whatever number you wish to speak in your brain, would have been raped, tortured and killed. Looking at the line of cars tonight I would have guessed at about the same number we killed tonight, maybe a few more, depending on children. We are killing those citizens of these United States who call themselves militia because they are nothing but murderers and rapists. Those people we have been killing are nothing better than rabid animals."

"Are you serious?"

"What the hell do you think we are doing here? We love this country. And we are trying to restore some sense of regular order to this part of the country by doing away with these rapists, child molesters and murderers. If they were not here, if this were not necessary we would be headed for Florida to fight the damned Cubans. Now tell us what the hell is going on in the real world?"

"What was going on when you came out here, Will?"

"As I was going up toward Cheyenne I saw the blooms of three devices that exploded over or around Omaha. I assumed SAC was taken out. Did Thunder Mountain get hit too?"

"Yes. But most of the missiles that were sent into the Minuteman fields of the Dakotas and eastern Montana were intercepted. It would not have made any difference. All of our missiles were launched by the time the Russian missiles arrived in the Dakotas. All of those that tried to hit the eastern population centers were intercepted with the exception of New York and Washington, D.C."

"A lot of Europe is gone. And most of the Russian Empire is gone, and most of the caliphate that the Sunnis were trying to build in Syria, Iraq, Iran, Afghanistan, and Pakistan is gone, especially on the Arabian Peninsula. Saudi Arabia and its oil fields, all of Iraq and Iran and their oil fields were destroyed by the Israelis. A lot of Israel is gone and its government has moved to Eilat down on the Red Sea Coast. All of the Islamist countries are no longer in existence for one reason or another. Riyadh, Teheran and Qum, Baghdad, Tikrit and Damascus, most of Lebanon were all taken out by the Israelis. Tel Aviv, Gaza, that whole area was hit by Iran. Iran does not exist except as a boiling mass of radioactive ground. India and Pakistan hit each other multiple times. Pakistan took the worst of it. You knew we had devastated Korea didn't you?"

"Yes, it happened just before I left on vacation. That was what it was meant to be I thought. But when I saw the blooms over Omaha I knew it had turned into something else. By the time I got up here it was what it was, the militia was trying to create its own government, steal everything it could use for its own benefit or whatever."

"Have you tried to talk to them, Will, or Mr. de Young," Jim asked?

"Who would we talk to?"

"You have some of their radios. I bet you could arrange a pow wow if you tried."

"You are wrong about them, Jim. But I will not be the one to burst your bubble. We will take you back to the rendezvous point tomorrow as planned. Why don't you and some of your people come up here and see if you can get to talk to them. Bring a couple of helicopters, bring some heavy stuff that you can use to impress them if you need to, maybe an M-48 tank or two. Because if you don't bring the heavy stuff you won't make it past the first meeting place which was compromised night before last. You do know your buddy Ken Stills was gutted by those people don't you?"

"No, I was not aware. But it changes nothing. The killing has to stop sooner than later. Things are getting better. We are restoring grid for electricity every day. We never lost any of our ability to generate electricity, we just lost transmission capability for a time. We have television up and rolling in a few places. The"front" is stabilized in northern Florida and we are preparing for a counter attack there. Our fleet is basically intact and we had all our boomers return, reload and go back to sea in case the Russians got friendly again. The Sixth Fleet in the Med was lost for the most part but all their aircraft were able to get back to land in Israel or Jordan. But the Seventh Fleet in the Indian Ocean is intact and fully operable. We are beginning to rock and roll all over the country. There are a few places like this where there are problems. We don't yet have enough military men back in harness and trained up to take care of those places by ourselves. But we are working toward getting enough. So are the State Patrol in Montana and Idaho."

"How many men do you have available to bring here, Jim?"

"Ken and I were it. But we thought we would be coming here to do some negotiations, restore the civil government, and get things back to normal."

"The last two Dad and I killed yesterday, did you notice Dad, they were covered in prison tats?"

"Yes and that probably means not only the county jails all over this part of the state have been emptied but so have the prisons. Still think you are here to restore the civil government, bring peace to the area through negotiation, Jim?"

"Okay, I give in. When do you sortie again?"

"This evening. It generally takes us about an hour or two to get to the killing fields. They are usually very evident. The militiamen are such idiots they just go to sleep on sentry status. There are generally anywhere from ten to twenty on sentry status. We eliminate them starting at one end until we find no more. Then we move down and attack those at the roadblock. And Jim, there has never been a night yet where there were not at least half a dozen cars of average people who made the mistake of getting off I-90 onto Hwy. 93. All the cars seem to have at least one child in them lately. We try to kill all the roadblock guards every night. We throw them all in the back of their pick-up trucks and light them afire in the hopes some of the rest will come out to see what is going on. We got four pick-ups and a Humvee the last time we had them come out. But they have stopped coming out to the roadblock. When they don't come out there they try to set some kind of trap for us in the forest with anywhere from three to five guys. We do them and then come on home with all the weapons, ammunition and cash we can carry."

"Jim," Dad said, "you being a Green Beret probably doesn't mean shit here frankly. If you have never served in a long range recon unit with the army in a combat situation your skills are in need of honing. Have you ever done long range recon, Jim?"

"Exactly what do you refer to Mr. de Young," asked Jim, a little ruffled by the directness of what dad had said, and then added, "No, I have not done long range recon."

"You'll see this evening. Let's get some rest."

We geared up in the evening, not so much for a sortie but for Jim's training. Dad said to him, "We will slip into the forest. We will be within five hundred yards of the house. It will be your job to find us. Do not go down the animal trail that you saw leading toward the house today. If you do we will have to be taking punji stakes out of you. So you have the area toward the forest from the trail, no less than one hundred feet or so from the trail into the trees please. Then you have the forest. We will not be together. Use your night vision. Walk carefully."

We left the house. Jim came out about fifteen minutes later as planned. He struck out into the forest and was making so much noise he couldn't hear himself think. He was only aware of his visual acuity in the first instance. After he had gone about fifty yards into the forest, Will had him in a hold that could have ended with Jim's throat cut. Will said to him, "Quiet down, go more slowly, walk more carefully." And then Will disappeared into the forest again. Within no more than ten steps Will was lost to Jim, who by then was embarrassed and a little panicky.

But he was game, I will say he was game. He struck off into the forest again. This time he moved a little more slowly but was still making so much noise he could hear nothing else around him but the noise he was making. Dad poked him in the butt with an arrow from a crossbow. As he turned toward dad, I took him back into the hold that would end with his throat slit. "Jesus, guys," he said, "how in the hell do you sneak up on me so easily?"

"You will learn, Jim," Dad said, and then ominously he said, "You will have to learn to stay here or you will die." We went back to the house. I took Jim with me out into the woods again. I showed him how slowly it was necessary to move and how much distance one could cover very slowly but seemingly in just a few seconds. We started back toward the house from about a mile into the woods. We were both covered in camo and our skins were painted the colors of the forest as well. I signaled him to shut up and sit down where he was.

The three of them were as arrogant as usual. One was smoking a cigarette. One was talking loudly on the radio to a woman. One was playing music through something like an iPod, and wearing an ear bug. They were spread out quite a bit. I took the one with the ear bud first because he was closest to me. He went down with a knife to the kidney and then his throat was cut and he bled out. The second one heard some of the movement of the first one's body I guess. He came weapons ready and I pinned him to a tree with the crossbow, shot him through the temple. He never moved. The third one didn't know I was following him until I sapped him. I needed a little information if he would cooperate.

When the guy awakened I had him trussed up in twist ties. And I had him gagged. I showed him the K-Bar up close and personal. I asked him if he intended to try and yell to some of his buddies. He shook his head no. I removed some of the gag. I asked him if there was anyone else out tonight except for the roadblock people. He was looking at that knife like it was a lie detector. He said no. I believed him. I asked him if he knew how many people were left in the militia. He said he didn't know for sure but he thought it was about fifty. I asked him if any of them had deserted and gone to other towns. He laughed at me and said "Hell yeah." I cut his throat. In a matter of minutes he was dead.

Jim wretched several times as I cut this one's throat. Finally he said, "How can you be so cold blooded?"

"This man probably raped at least twenty women, killed at least twenty of our citizens for no reason other than they made the mistake of getting on Hwy. 93. He did not deserve to live."

"It's so simple to you. These guys are rapists and murderers and they deserve what they get," Jim asked.

"It's very simple," I responded. Then I said "Are you all done for the evening or do you want to go with me to the roadblock and blood yourself?"

"No, I don't think I can do it tonight. Can we go back to the house now?" We did.. When we got there, dad and I left, went to the road-block and did our usual number there. This time we brought back another SAW and another light machine gun. We also brought back some photos we took of the cars that evening. There were only four but all four had at least two and one had three kids in it. The kids were all girls. They had all been raped, mutilated and murdered along with their parents. When we unloaded the weapons in the spider holes we showed Jim the pictures. He ran for the bathroom again.

"I have a feeling," I said to dad, "Jim is not going to be of much use to us, dad. The guy I interrogated tonight told me there were about fifty left in the militiamen's group. It might not hurt to do some snip-ing from good vantage points from which we can get into a hidey hole immediately in order to avoid the helicopters. That might further encourage some more of them to desert. Some have already deserted according to the guy I talked to tonight."

"I will work with Jim," my father told me. "There is a fifty caliber down in the cave. You might want to try shooting it a few times before we think about using it to do some sniping. Of course there is always the old standby Remington 700 down there as well. Try both and see what you think you want to do. In the meantime I will see if I can get Jim to quiet down in the woods a little."

We decided in the evening we would go down to an area on a small hillside overlooking the town and I would set up a sniping position. We did and I picked off several of them going in and out of the police station before I heard a helicopter coming my direction. I buried up in a small rocky area that gave me the option of shooting as well. I had brought an RPG with me. As the helicopter flew slowly over the area I was hiding in I fired the RPG at the helo and ran like hell away from that spot. Luckily I hit the helo pretty hard apparently and it limped off toward the city airport.

About the same time Jim and dad were broadcasting to the militia, asking them to consider a negotiation, an end to the hostilities rather than continue with the war. The resultant response of the other helicopter firing its machine guns at the spot from which they seemed to be sending their radio messages told us everything we needed to know about that issue. A few stupid ones tried to come into the forest to look for Jim and dad. They were dispatched to their own Valhalla in various ways by dad. Jim did not assist once again.

The next night was a meeting night for the State Police set up and when they left from the meeting Jim left with them but one of the State Police boys, also a former Recon Marine, came back with us. His name was Allan Coxey. Allan is a man of about five feet eight inches in height and probably weighs close to one hundred ninety pounds. I could see there was no fat on this man though. I thought he would do just fine.

Allan volunteered to take up rear end charlie in our walk back to the house. As usual we were using ear buds and radios but only squelch transmissions. One transmission meant enemy in the area. Two meant imminent danger. Three meant duck and cover and hope like hell. Allan gave us a two squelch transmission. We went to ground. We heard some grunting. Soon Allan came along with two more M-16 rifles, two more silenced pistols, a crossbow with arrows and a pack full of money. When we saw him and saw that it was clear, we exposed ourselves.

He nearly jumped out of his skin when dad stepped out of the trees right next to him. "Shit," he said, "You scared me half to death. There are no more back there." He took his knife out and cleaned it in the dirt for a moment. Now, both dad and I knew that Allan Coxey was a man to be reckoned with, and he would not have the same personal outlook as that of Jim Martinez. Then we continued toward the house.

After we were home, cleaned up and sat down to eat something, after all the greetings and introductions Allan said to my dad, "Major, I am sorry about sending you the army guy. He turned out to be worthless I guess. I am in charge of the few of us that are in Missoula. There is a grand total of three now that Ken is dead. Jim Martinez is one of them and the other is Marty Jimson."

"I know, Marty," dad said, "how is that old reprobate?"

"You know, Major, that is exactly what Marty said would be your response. He is fine and looking forward to coming out and spending some time with you. We think it best from our operational point of view if we alternate personnel in and out about once a week if it is okay with you."

"Allan," Dad asked, "was your father a Captain in my Recon battalion headquarters?"

"Yes sir, he was. And he sent his greetings as well. He has a broken leg unfortunately or he would be here now. But yes he was. He is chomping at the bit to get out here and 'git some.'"

"By God, it's good to have another marine here," my dad said. I just mouthed the word Hooraw. We all laughed. But it was good to have another man we didn't have to train, who probably knew as much about the woods and moving through them as we did. And Alan was a little younger than either dad or I. Damn it was good. We talked a lot about our inventory of weapons at that point.

"Do you have any small shoulder mounted ground to air stuff that won't raise a dust cloud big enough for a man five miles away to see? I would like to shoot that other helicopter down if I could. If that could be done we can do some stand off shooting and reduce their numbers even further than they are now."

"When I go back I will see what I can scrounge up, sir," Allan said. "Everything is in a little bit of a short supply right now as you can well understand. But progress is being made in Florida, the Cubans are getting their asses handed to them after insertion of the marines into the front lines. The Cubans don't like either the Cobras or the army war birds, the Apaches. They are getting hit from every angle with those now. Supply must be hellatious for them. The fleet has shut off the island from Florida. The Cuban Air Force no longer exists, their missile defense systems were destroyed by weasels and HARM's in the last week or so I understand. There was a rumor going around Miami last week when I was doing recon there the Castros are making an attempt to communicate with us in hopes of achieving a cease fire before all their troops are slaughtered."

"Goddamn it," Dad said, just as mom walked into the room, "I was kind of hoping to get over there and get a taste of that one too."

"Like hell you will, Eugene de Young," she said. "You have your own personal little war to fight and it's not done yet. When you finish this one you will be all done with war, mister. I can tell you for sure about your fighting days. So get that damn Cuban thing out of your mind."

He looked a little sheepish but he damned sure didn't argue with his wife of so many years. She invited us all to have coffee and donuts and we agreed. Bed was beckoning to me. Ruthie and I went to bed, leaving the boys to mom, right after the donuts which were home made. Damn my mother can definitely cook. And damn my wife can definitely make love and knows when it is needed and appropriate for me even if not for her necessarily. I love her to the nth degree. I try to make sure every day she knows how much I love her in some small way. On the night when Alan came it was with a crashing moment of bliss for her as well as for me. But the best moment of the day was just before sleep in which we both started to kiss each other and say at the same time "Do you know much I love you?"

Chapter 8

War Comes to an End

The practice of sleeping during the day and fighting at night was wearing on the women. I could not blame either one of them particularly for being a little testy from time to time. They were always with the kids, and always on the alert to any activity around the house. They were our guardians in the day while we were theirs in the night. It was difficult for them. Going outside was dangerous, maybe, but how to know when it was true? They were not marines after all.

Sometimes they were outside with the kids playing various games in the light of day while they could. One day while they were not paying enough attention to the sounds around them a helicopter pulled up out of the trees and spotted them almost instantly.

Of course they ran toward the house, but they were quite a distance away from the house when they started to run. They were pretty near to a spider hole though, and mom knew where it was located. Now what are you going to do if you are the pilot of a gunship and see a bunch of targets running away from you? What do you think he did? He fired on them as he should have.

And he awakened dad, and I as he did so. The kids were first into the hole. The women barely made it before the machine guns chewed up dirt all around them. They closed the hole and ran for the house. Dad and I picked up two RPG's when we realized what was happening and went up one hole closer to the house.

The helicopter was hovering in the area of the canyon, looking, trying to figure out what the hell it had seen and what to do next. He was probably talking on the radio at the same time. In either case he didn't see dad and I come out of the spider hole and go behind trees, preparing to fire at him. His view of us was partially blocked by the house itself. The two RPG's hit the front of the helicopter almost simultaneously. The explosion was huge and blew a hell of a hole in the aircraft. It did a kind of slow roll to the right and then went straight down into the bottom of the canyon where there was another huge explosion.

"Well," I said, "it looks like we won't be bothered with helicopters any longer unless they bring in another one from somewhere else."

We went back inside. Allan had barely awakened and come outside to see what happened when we were on the way back into the house. He said, "What happened?"

"Nothing much," Dad said, "we just shot down their other helicopter. It spotted the women and kids outside and fired at them so we shot it down. Two more of them have bitten the dust." We had a tote board in the edge of the cave as you went in there from the house. Dad marked two more on it. There was well over a hundred marks there now. War is hell, what can I say? No regrets, for sure, and why would there be with those idiots?

Then came the moment we had all dreaded. The radios we had confiscated from the militiamen we had killed all came on with an announcement at the same time. "This is Col. Wayne Powers of the New

Montana Militia. I am Eileen Powers' nephew. You killed my Aunt you assholes. And now we know where you are, who you are, what you are. We are coming de Youngs, we are coming. And you will not be able to stop us. We will capture you, we will torture you and we will kill you with great pleasure. It won't be today, but maybe tomorrow, who knows. But we are coming assholes." About the moment that he finished RPG rounds began to fall all around the compound, on top of the house, everywhere in the area.

One of our spider hole openings was hit. It was the one the women and kids had gone down, nearly the most remote from the house. It was not a great loss if the tunnel was destroyed. We couldn't tell if that was true yet. The barrage of grenades ended after about twenty minutes.

We went down the tunnels to see what if any damage existed. There was none. Only the one door to the outside world had been hit and it was hardly damaged, hardly moved from its original location by the explosion. We could see out the aperture. Powers had lied to us. They were coming. Some were coming through the forest, from the west almost directly, some from the northwest toward Arlee, and some directly down the animal trail.

There were about twenty of them in the trees to the west that I could see. There were about twenty of them coming from the northwest and about twenty more coming on the animal trail. The center mass of men was just about in the middle of the trail area, not spread out very well and really vulnerable. Dad waited until they were within the kill zone of the claymores and then loosed hell on them. All were wounded or killed. All of them! It was an amazing moment. But the other forty or so did not know what had happened and they kept on coming.

The twenty or so of them coming from the west had some automatic weapons. And they were spraying fire into the area of our home as fast as they could do so. Some of them were on ATV's and were firing SAW's at us. One of the groups of about ten of those men was near to the firing aperture of a spider hole containing one of the light machine guns we had captured. I killed them all with four bursts from that gun. The other ten went to ground because they could not tell where the firing was coming from that was killing their comrades.

The twenty or so coming from the northeast were idiots. Most of them, as it turned out, were released prisoners from the Montana State Prison system. They had no idea what they were facing. Allan took them on single handedly with two SAW's that we had prepared and ready in that area. They started to lob grenades at the area of the house. None of them hit the house itself. None of them harmed anything.

Every time some of them would try to move forward or stand up to lob grenades Allan would kill them. He wasted little ammunition firing in bursts of three to six rounds at a time, hitting every target he acquired. He was in an aperture on the Northeast side of the house they could not see. By the time they got close enough to the house to see what they were facing there were only three of those men left that were not wounded or dead.

The ten that remained in the woods to the west were mine. I prepped for the job by putting on the standard forest outfit dad and I had been using from the outset of the contest with these wing nuts. It was beginning to get full dark when I slipped out of the spider hole closest to the ten that were left. They had remained in roughly the same position as when I was killing their comrades from the spider hole aperture. They had tried to form a little perimeter they could maintain through the night. They were periodically shining lights in the direction of the house to see if anything was moving.

But it was too late for the lights they were using to do them any good because I was already behind them. I took the one furthest away from the rest for my first shot with the bow. He was hit in the back of the head. He never made a sound. Someone called to the guy and when he didn't answer came crawling over to see where the guy was. He died similarly. There was no sport in this, no honor, nothing but kill or be killed. Yes, I thought, from time to time, we might be more violent than the militia. Our brand of violence was not visited on the innocent was the only response I could make. Oh yes there was one more thing. Our brand of violence would end when the militia was ended.

The next guy was a little closer in to the perimeter. I had to be careful with him because he was already nervous as hell and was yelling at his buddies all the time, "What's going on, I cannot see anything, what's going on?"

In the midst of one of those sentences he died with another arrow from the crossbow. His words were chopped off and that alerted the group leader. He started yelling for the guy and then yelling for the other three. By the time he began to yell at the others I had moved away from being directly behind them, knowing they might spray that area with gunfire. They did. Three of them fired to the front, toward the house, and the other four fired toward the forest. None of their shots came close to me but my silenced pistol took out the leader in the middle of all that noise. I also got one other I thought might be a leader as well. Five more remained alive.

Those five broke and ran. I shot one within two feet of me. Another saw me and started to turn toward me when an arrow appeared through his head. I knew dad was out there then. The last guy to run saw dad apparently, and started shooting at him. I shot that guy about six times with the MP-5 I was carrying. The last one of them threw his weapon to the ground and fell down, screaming at the top of his lungs, 'don't shoot, don't shoot'." I trussed him up with twist ties and took him to the animal trail.

Those who were badly wounded there we simply shot in the head. I let our prisoner watch me do them. I wanted him even more scared than he had been earlier. There was nowhere to take their wounded and dead and no one to take care of them outside the town. We didn't know if the hospital, hell it was just a small clinic, had any personnel left or not. We doubted it would be true. We were right in the end and we were not going there yet.

After the twenty for which I had responsibility were thrown off the cliff's edge those who had died on the animal trail were put on the back of one of the ATV's and the same happened to them. Most of those on the northwest side of the house that Allan had killed were very close to the cliff. He threw them over the cliff as we were doing with the rest. The total of the attacking force was over sixty, all dead save for one.

All my dad ever said about the entire thing was "Well, sometimes a fortress has a chance of survival. That chance comes if the enemy seeking to vanquish the fortress is so stupid that they attack it frontally. I'm sure that if there are any of them left now they won't make that mistake again. So let's find out how many of them are left."

I had made a small fire to heat my knife. It was good and hot, red steel in color when I showed it to my prisoner. I stood him up, stripped off his pants and took off his shorts with the knife itself, burning his legs just a little bit. I said to him at that point, "I am only going to ask this question one time and if I get a smartass answer or an 'I don't know', or anything other than a number, I will cut off your right testicle slowly. It will hurt like hell. Then I will ask again. Do you get the drift?"

He nodded his head. I said to him, "How many are there left in your little army son?"

He started to say "I don't..." then stopped and said "forty I think, maybe thirty-five but right around that number I think. Most of us came out here today."

"Good. Now let's move on to the next question. Where are you storing all your weapons or do you carry them around with you all the time?"

Again he started to say "I don't..." and then he said "some of us carry them with us. Most do not. Most of the weapons are in the barracks all the time."

"Where is the barracks you are talking about lad?"

"It was the State Police Barracks before..."

"You are doing great. Now where is your headquarters, where your leaders stay all the time unless they are with you in an attack?"

"It's in the library. Mrs. Powers was kind of our leader before she got killed. Her son also got killed so her nephew took over. He was with us today so he is dead also I guess."

"Who is your next leader in line?"

"She is a teacher from our high school. Boy is she a tough one. She started to get higher in the group by, you know, by having sex with the leaders. Then she was a leader. Now she is the only one left. All the rest are dead. They were all with us on this attack."

"How did you find out where we were located?"

"When the helicopter saw the women and kids outside it sent us messages back before you shot it down."

"Do you have any heavy weapons?"

"I don't know what you mean by that, sir," he responded. I cut off his right testicle. He screamed for a long time. Mom brought him an ice bag and put it on the wound and he calmed down a little. I asked him again. He said "We don't have any mortars or artillery, anything like that, no, and we used up the last of the RPG's we had just before we attacked your house. Goddamn, what the hell is that house made of?"

I asked him "Where are your sentries located in the perimeter of the town, in spider holes or in the houses that are boarded up?"

"They are in the houses which are boarded up. They have little spaces left that they can look out and shoot out."

"How long have they been in the boarded up houses?"

"Only for the last day or two."

"How many of them are there?"

"I don't know."

"That is unfortunate" I said and I cut off his left testicle. Apparently that one hurt more than the other one. He screamed even louder and a little more in a soprano voice when the second one went. (A joke, just a little joke). Again mom came out and put an ice bag on him. I said "How many sentries are there?"

"Oh God," he said.

"No, just Will de Young, you little bastard. Now answer the question or I will cut off your little dick so you will have to squat to pee. Do you hear me?"

"Yes, sir. There are at least six of them. They rotate houses though. I cannot tell you which houses they are using. It depends on who is on sentry which house they want to use. Some of them are couples and I think they use those places to have sex since no one is threatening the town. I know it is what my girlfriend and I did when we served sentry duty."

"All right boy. Last question. What time do your people go to sleep?"

"Usually the town closes down at around 9:00 p.m. and everyone's lights are out by ten. The curfew hour is ten o' clock. No one is allowed outside after ten o' clock."

"Okay, son." I cut off the twist ties and told him to pull up his pants. Most of the blood flow had been staunched by the hot blade and the ice bags. But he was still bleeding a little. "You better head home now boy. Remember my face well for if ever you see it again for on he day you see me again you will most certainly die. Do you understand me clearly?"

"Yes, sir. I will get medical attention before I leave town and then I am gone, sir. Thank you for letting me live."

"Don't make me regret my choice boy. If I were to capture you again you would live for hours in the kind of pain you felt here today, you understand me?"

"Yes, sir," he said as he began to walk away.

My dad yelled at the boy, "Don't go on the trail. Go through the forest the way you came. If you go on the trail you will die."

Allan and my dad had watched all this occurring. "Based on what the boy said I think it's time to go on the offensive, dad."

"I agree," he said, "but with care and with direct objectives that are simple and easy to accomplish."

"Jesus you sounded just like a lecture I once received in the Recon school, sir," Allan said to dad. All I could do was nod because I too had heard those very words in Recon school.

"It is probably because your instructor was once one of my students. He probably picked the saying up from me exactly as I just said it. This is not the first time I have uttered those words to Recon Marines."

"All right then," I said, "what should be our initial objectives? We have taken the initiative away from them today I think. Even though they know where we are they know they don't have enough people and enough experience to take us on out here."

Allan spoke up and said, "If I were in command I would want to continue to knock down their leadership structure and attack their core in their realm where they think they are safe."

"How are you at playing God, Allan?" my father asked.

"Jesus, Mary and Joseph, don't tell me you have a fifty caliber sniper's rifle. But if you do I am very experienced with it. I acted as 'God' for a couple of different Seal activities, in fact. In answer to your question, sir, and I do mean sir. Major, what is it you need my son?"

We all had to laugh at that one but it was wonderful for me. I hated that damn cannon. "Wow, that's great, that blunderbuss just shakes me up so badly that I cannot hit anything with it. Good. Then what we could do, dad, is eliminate the sentries out in the forest, if there are any, as we have been doing, eliminate the roadblock and have Allan come in behind us by an hour or so and set up to watch the barracks and shoot anyone that goes in or out. What do you think of that, dad? Allan?"

"Sounds good to me" they both said. "Let's get some rest now. Tonight is going to be hell on wheels I expect. If they don't attack us we will definitely attack them. I don't think they have the balls for a night attack." So it was. Rest is one of the most important features of being a guerilla. Without sufficient rest it is easy to be less than focused and to make a mistake which costs lives. We were in bed about two o' clock in the afternoon and up at around eight thirty in the evening. Nothing had disturbed the area of the house as far as we could tell. We had done a lot of repair work in the day before going to bed to make sure that the scars left by the RPG's were gone and the place looked as natural as it had before the attack.

We geared up and left the house by about nine thirty. We moved slowly and quietly through the woods as usual. Allan stayed at the house and would leave there an hour after us unless we came hot footing it back as a result of a pending attack being formed. We did not find any attack coming. We did find a half dozen sentries that we eliminated. We eliminated the four on the roadblock as well, did our usual number with the trucks and waited to see if any of them would come out. They did not. Allan arrived just about the time we were going to slip back into the forest. We took him to a good sniper's locale for the barracks and set him up. Dad stayed with him as a spotter. I wanted to do a little more recon.

The lights around the perimeter of the town were on stands set up into the air some twenty five feet or so. I shot out three of them to create a dark spot. They wouldn't know the lights were out unless they were awake and alert. I went to one of the houses that was boarded up along the front street. I listened for a time and heard snoring. I slipped into the house through an opening it was obvious the sentry was using. No one stopped me or yelled at me. I shot two sentries in that house.

I went to the next house in the line of those in the dark spot, found two more sentries, heard a massive boom in the forest and heard the sound of a fifty caliber round striking home just at about the same time I was ridding the world of the two in the house I had entered. I ventured far enough into the inner ring of the town to see a body in front of the barracks. I also saw someone peeking out the door and the windows to see if anyone was around.

He finally decided it was okay, came out to see about his buddy and died in the same spot from the massive impact of a fifty caliber bullet in the chest area. He was moved about two feet by the kinetic energy of the round. All the lights came on in the barracks. Someone came running out to see about their buddies while shooting was directed at the forest from a lot of the windows of the building. The third one died on the spot and I picked off two in the windows who were back lit and shooting in Allan's general direction. The shooting stopped. Another guy poked his head out the door far enough to look at the bodies. He died from a shot that struck him in the middle of his body after going through part of the wall. The shooting started again and I picked off another couple of them. Then I hauled it on out of town back to where my dad and Allan were located.

As I ran out of town the rounds they were firing from the barracks were all going way high over my head and over the head of my dad and Allan. I got back to where they were and said "I got six and you got four and that leaves them with at most about twenty people considering those we took in the forest and at the roadblock. I bet they lose some to desertion tomorrow. I bet this war is just about over." We stayed a little longer that evening because we were going to take Allan to the rendezvous point.

We watched the people that were left come out in two pick-up trucks and look for their sentries in the houses. They brought them out and put them in the back of the truck. They sent two guys into the forest to look for the sentries. We killed them. The other two went to the roadblock. We killed them. It was like shooting fish in a barrel. We took out twenty-four of their people in one night. Three of us had eliminated two entire companies of troops in numbers and most of those were killed by two of us.

We went to the rendezvous site and met with the State Police. I thought if they had at least six people they could most likely take the barracks. They asked what time of day would be best and I said about ten o' clock at night. They left and Allan stayed with us. We snuck into town through the darkened area and went to the barracks to see if anyone was awake. We looked in through windows with our night vision devices and didn't see anyone. We did see a few weapons laying around. As usual we policed those up and headed out of town with all our latest installment of loot.

We had a huge surprise at the house when we got home nearing dawn. Mom and Ruthie were sitting in the living room of the house. They were sipping coffee and waiting for us to get there. Mom didn't say a word, she got up, crooked her finger at us and went down the stairs to the cave. In the cave were two men. One was tied up and gagged, the other was tied up. They had used twist ties and they had tied them so tightly there was blood coming from the wrists and legs. "Who are they?" dad asked.

"One of them said he was the son of the guy that said he was Eileen's nephew. He was the latest leader of the group according to him. He must be all of fifteen years old. The other one is the son of the school teacher the other kid talked about. He is fifteen I think."

"Did they come armed," I asked.

"No. They came walking up to the house with their hands in the air and begged us not to shoot them. We tied their hands behind them one at a time and then brought them down here and tied them up completely."

I said to the boy who was Eileen's nephew's son, "What is your name, son?"

"Jimmy, sir, Jimmy Lyons. My father was married to Eileen's daughter for a while."

"How old are you?"

"Fifteen, sir."

"How often did you work the roadblock son?"

"Never, sir. Never. They wouldn't let us work out there. They said it was too dangerous. But we heard what they were doing and we didn't want to work out there anyway."

"What's your buddy's name here?"

"Waylon."

"How old is Waylon?"

"Fifteen also, sir. We worked together in the group."

"How did you get involved in all this shit kid?"

"Waylon's mom was involved from the get-go, sir. That was how. I was living with them. My mom is dead and my dad ran off a couple of years ago. Waylon's mom and dad let me live with them."

"What was your job Jimmy, you and Waylon?"

"We did two things every day, sir. We counted the money and we cleaned weapons."

"Now the critical questions young man. The answers you give now, and how you react to these questions as we all watch you, may well determine whether you live or die. I don't want to have to kill you. But lie to me, try to lure me into a trap, put my family in danger and you will die very quickly. Do I make myself perfectly clear?"

"Yes, sir." He began to cry a little at that point. He said, "I'm sorry, sir. I couldn't contain myself." A puddle formed at his feet, his pants were wet all the way to his crotch. He had definitely peed on himself he was so afraid.

"Okay, Jimmy, who is left in the barracks?'

"No one, sir. We were the last two to leave town. The rest of them took off this morning."

"How many were there that took off?"

"Three I think, no maybe four. I think there were four, yes, sir."

"What did they drive when they left town?"

"A blue pick-up truck, sir. It was full of weapons and money in the bed, sir. The money was all baled up. That was part of my job with Waylon here, to bale the money in large bales like hay."

"How many of the people that we have killed came from Arlee or Alberton?"

"I'm not lying to you, sir, I really don't know for sure. But I think most of the guys that were fighting or got killed out at the roadblock were from Arlee. We only had maybe fifty guys from Frenchtown join the militia, sir. Most of the people from here ran off the first day of the war, sir. They headed for Portland and Seattle I think. Or maybe for somewhere else in Montana."

"So as far as you know there are no other militiamen waiting in Frenchtown for us?"

"Not anyone I know of, sir."

"Fair enough. We will see tomorrow. Mom, why don't you feed these two lads something? And when you feed them you can cut them loose outside. If there are any stray militiamen out there the boys will be our early warning device. The militiamen will shoot them first before trying to get into the house."

Allan had a satellite phone that he used to communicate with the State Police if necessary. He had brought it with him when he joined us a couple of days earlier. A couple of days? Was it all that had passed since he came to help us? It seemed as though he had been there forever. He called and told them to come to the town the next morning. He said we would all be set up as sniper's to provide them with cover and if they did not need cover we would go on home and talk to them later.

As we set up at three separate locations to act as snipers the blue pick-up truck that Jimmy had told us about returned from the direction of Arlee. It had six people in it. We didn't want to have the State Police run into an ambush. I squelched three times and we took them out. Dad and Allan took the three in the back of the truck. I took the three in the front of the truck. The passengers went first and then the driver. The truck was stopped and he was trying to bail out when I shot him. We left them where they lay with their weapons so the Statie's could see what they would have had to deal with.

Two of them had SAW's and the others all had M-16's and they had a lot of ammunition. We took most of that. We left a note for the State Police that there were no more militiamen and headed back to the house.

We confiscated three ATV's. When we got home Allan unloaded all his weapons, gave us all the ammo and money he had taken off the guys in town and said goodbye to mom, Ruthie and the kids and headed back for town. We all wished him well and knew he was likely headed for Florida. Our war was over. Or at least so I thought. Or at least so we all thought, Allan included.

We had defeated a militia. They were not real military men. They did not understand the realities of war.
Water shapes its course according to the nature of the ground over which it flows. The soldier works out his victory in relation to the foe he is facing.
Sun Tzu, The Art of War

BOOK II
DEVASTATION,
MONEY TALKS,
WAR STARTS AGAIN

In the Midst of Chaos there is also Opportunity
Sun Tzu, The Art of War

Chapter 9

We Assess, Reassess and Wait

When the war with the Frenchtown militiamen, those who called themselves the Army of northwestern Montana, ended, we had an arsenal at our disposal. We had confiscated from those casualties we created over fifty pistols, mostly Beretta nine millimeter and about half of those were equipped with silencers. In addition we had taken over one hundred and fifty AR-15 and M-16 or M-4 rifles, half a dozen SAW weapons, three light machine guns and one fifty caliber machine gun. We also had confiscated more than twenty RPG launchers and over fifty rifle grenades.

When dad and I took inventory of the stuff we had taken off those people we were surprised at the totals but not surprised at the lethality of the weapons they had been able to commandeer. Plus their money supplies were the banks, until they ran dry of currency. One more source they had for money, of course, being the people they killed.

The cemetery in Frenchtown was filled up with bodies in shallow graves. God knows how many there were. The State Police thought it would be unable to identify half of them through any means but did find a body of driver's licenses thrown into a box in the barracks. Of course the driver's licenses did not give us a count of the children below the age of holding a driver's license. But from that bunch of driver's licenses the State Police decided the total number of murder victims of the militia had to be over a thousand.

There was no way to know for sure the money we confiscated came from the victims of murder or from the banks. There was no way to determine how to get it back to its "rightful owners" if there were any left. All the banks in Arlee, Frenchtown and Alberton had long ago closed their doors. No one knew where the owners, operators, leaders of those institutions had gone, no one knew anything which could give us a way to return the money. So we kept it. In the run of time it was a good decision.

It turned out that the militia we fought was only one of a number that tried to take control of various areas of Washington, Oregon, Montana, Idaho, northern California, parts of Utah and Wyoming and most of Kansas and Nebraska as well as other pockets in other states like Arizona, Nevada and New Mexico. I guess the worst of the militia fights eventually took place in Texas. After the Cuban incursion into Florida had been beaten back and the Cuban forces decimated almost to a man the army forces fought and killed hundreds of militiamen in Texas who had seized control of some areas of the Lone Star state.

Our assessment, in learning other areas were still fighting their militias, was that those kinds of wars would prove to be more devastating in the run of time to the population of the country than the nuclear attacks. Later we would discover our thoughts were pretty much correct. We were right even though the large part of the population did survive everything, including the militia wars. Don't get me wrong.

Millions died in the nuclear exchange and millions more died in the militia wars.

Normalcy, whatever you want to call it, just because the war with our militia was over, had not been reestablished in the country as a whole. Nor was it completely so in our own area. Up near Arlee the militiamen who were left there went into hiding further north into the panhandle of Idaho where many of their brethren were located. But a few continued to set roadblocks in strange places and continued their murdering, raping and thieving ways.

The barter system had begun to replace currency in some places, we were told. It was not true in Missoula/Frenchtown. It was said a nine millimeter bullet was worth more than a hundred dollar bill in many places. Everything was by word of mouth except for what little we got from Radio USA. Rumor mongering was a pastime for almost everyone. Our rumors were not about people so much as about our circumstances. The militia war changed everything. When it was over the time came to change things back to "normal." But what had become the norm was unknown in many respects.

RUSA was mostly broadcasting news of the battles in Florida. The news from Florida was good. The fighting there was basically over. The Cubans were fools to try and invade. They lost their most elite forces. The Cubans were brave and good fighters. But they were no match for our fire power and our troops.

Those of us who had plenty of currency in our hands were generally without worries as to supplies. As soon as Hwy. 90 and I-15 were completely open to traffic supplies began to flow to us from the cities of Oregon and Washington, from Utah and Canada and from California to a degree. We even began to get some produce into the stores that were reopening in Missoula and Frenchtown. The produce came from Mexico and was being imported through Arizona.

It turned out that the farming areas in northern California had not shut down at all. Salinas operated at full bore producing its array of "produce" for both its own state and the other states of the northwest, to whatever places it could be distributed safely. And Arizona was sending out fairly sizable amounts of its crops, lettuce, hay, and other forms of produce to those places that could afford to buy. The hay, of course, was used for silage in some places but mostly to feed the few cattle we could round up and pen so the markets could begin to provide meat to the remaining population. Eastern Montana had been a ranching area since the establishment of longhorn cattle from Texas by the passage over the Gallup Trail. But no one was going into eastern Montana because of the nuclear attacks in the northeastern quadrant of the state. No one really knew whether militias controlled the southeast of the state or not. Chicken farming began right away after the nuclear exchange. In Missoula a kind of cooperative effort built large pens for chickens. There were also a few cattle ranches around the area. So meat supplies, though not abundant, were available if one had the price. Everything was expensive. One cannot blame those selling for the prices. No one knew from one day to the next what was going to happen. Everyone survived as best they could.

So the first few weeks after the "war" of Frenchtown was over were given in terms of our time to the reestablishment of the defensive systems around our "fortress." There was also addition of a few newer ideas based on the battles we had fought in that area. We tried to get to a point where we could go down to Missoula, only fifteen miles from us to get news or supplies. Did we give up any of the weapons we had confiscated? No.

Did we give up any of the ammunition that we had amassed? If you say that using ammunition to trade is "giving it up" then yes we did. But not a lot of any one caliber, especially not a lot of .223 caliber, that is used in the light machine guns, the SAW's and the M-4's, M-16's and AR-15's. We had lined up walls full of rifles, SAW's, all the stuff we had taken away from those yokels and box after box of loaded clips of ammunition for every type of weapon we had. We would not let go of that for some time to come. But forty-five caliber bullets and some thirty caliber bullets were used to barter for various food stuffs. Mostly we froze everything we could. But boy was it a treat to get a head of lettuce or a couple of tomatoes or a dozen eggs; yes, real eggs.

Were we supposed to give up those guns, the ammunition, the machine guns, the ammunition canisters and boxes? Technically I suppose we should have done it. But we had been through a month of hell. We had killed over one hundred fifty men and boys, some rather brutally. We had fought day and night to save ourselves, our family, and our way of life. We were not about to let the government know what we had amassed as a result of our fight. Why should we? Though we were not prescient in any respect we had an inkling the militia wars had not ended. In fact, as it turned out, we were right.

There was no guarantee the bastards who had run away would not come back with a lot more men and try again. So we kept what we had, we hoped never to use it again, we hoped against hope things would get better and some idiot would not try to take over the area again. Remember the old saying of wish in one hand and crap in the other and see which fills up first. It had a lot of meaning for us in a rather short time frame.

A week or so after the battles were over I went down to Charley and Berneice's place. I thought sure my car would have been discovered and torched or maybe driven off somewhere to take the gasoline if nothing else. But lo and behold it was where I left it, the gas was still in the car, the clothes and everything were still in the trunk. There was a road dad finally showed me which came within about a half a mile from the house. It was what the militiamen had used to get into position to attack us from the southwest.

After we finally were able to bury Charlie and Berneice I drove my car back out there, unloaded my stuff and packed it to the house. It was an amazing feeling to have all my clothing, to have all my shaving gear, everything I had brought from D.C. with me at last. I felt almost whole, almost like I had arrived home, finally.

The reality of the situation continued to be somewhat less than the optimum for sure. There were no telephones, either cell or land line. The tel-satellites which had been in orbit at the time of the nuclear attacks had been, in part, destroyed by EMP blasts in space set off by one force or the other, either the U.S., the Russians, the Iranians, the Israelis, the North Koreans, the French, the English, the Pakistanis. All the nuclear powers had taken part in the war. All had suffered extreme devastation and one of the ways in which all of us were most heavily affected had to do with communications. The whole thing had gone on a little longer than I was aware. Some of those involved, like the Iranians, were not very smart about their future, or the future of the rest of the world.

Another way in which we were devastated and would have to work for years to overcome was in respect to the distribution of electric power. The state of Nebraska had been one of the hubs of the electric grid. The infrastructure was just simply vaporized in many places. The wires, the large towers (poles) that held the wiring did not exist in many areas of Nebraska. And the redirection of the electric grid could not be completely accomplished without some or all of that infrastructure being replaced or repaired. So electricity was still a matter of generators which were run largely from gasoline. That meant, of course, not many hours of the day were given to electric power generation because the amount of gasoline available was finite. Wind farming and solar generation existed in some places but the numbers of mega watts generated there was not sufficient for the entire nation.

Pipelines carrying "natural" gas from almost anywhere to anywhere in the U.S. had been the rule before the nuclear strikes. What was left of the pipeline system, no one seemed to know. According to what we were hearing substantial repair or replacement of those vital systems would take whatever amount of time it would take. Quien sabes (who knew)?

It began to be bandied about that laborers, workers in general, were in short supply. A lot of people had been murdered on the highways. A lot of people had been murdered in small towns like Frenchtown. A lot of militias had been broken down by attrition of their numbers through people like me killing them. So where were the workers going to come from? Who was going to operate the backhoes, the trench diggers, the clamps that installed the heavy and unwieldy pieces of pipe into the trench? Who was going to do the welding to insure the pipes did not leak? Skilled labor was not exactly jumping out of the woodwork for these projects. Everyone was still a little scared.

Some were afraid a group of gang members or militia type people would attack them and they wouldn't be able to defend themselves if they were away from their homes. Some were afraid to carry weapons if they had them. Having a weapon in an area where there was civil control reestablished was tantamount to being a militia type or a gang member. And in the large cities like Chicago and Cleveland the gangs held more control in the night than did the police and the army. In those places the authorities were still trying to make things work the way they had prior to the attack on our country.

Our reestablishment of the country as it had been would have to wait according to some. We were among those whose attitude was "go to war," finish off the opposition, if it's a gang, if it's a militia no matter. Kill as many as you can, take their weapons, strip them down to a few who have to run or die. There could be no disagreement with the attitude designed to end the militias in those early days. A harsh attitude was a necessity when it came to the murderers, the rapists, the Militias became.

On my first trip into Missoula of course I went armed. When I got to the State Police roadblock on Hwy. 90 they recognized me and let me go through without confiscating my weapons. Confiscation of weapons was what they were trying to do with everyone after the militia war in Frenchtown. But they let me through without a hitch. What it told me was they trusted me not to attack them or the banks or other people indiscriminately. Maybe it is how we should have been looking at each other earlier, before the nuclear attacks.

Weapons not in the hands of a madman cannot be used for the mad schemes that one dreams up. If you give him a gun he will use it to commit a crime. Once the crime is committed he will buy another in order to be able to commit a larger crime. That was the premise upon which the State Police and the Army were going. The proof of their reliance on those basic ideas lay in the militias.

There had to be some exceptions to those rules, though. Local cops had to be able to have guns, didn't they? When the State Police, my dad and Allan and his friends sat down to talk about these topics we tried to come up with exceptions which made sense. We left scratching our heads about the entire conversation and wondering what we had accomplished. I knew it was nothing.

Guns, the reliance on guns to solve problems in our society has been an issue since the earliest days of our national existence. The construct of a national army in those early days threatened the smaller states especially. Those smaller states did not want a large standing army to be formed by the central government. They had seen that under the British and it was in part what had caused the revolution.

They, those representing the small states like Rhode Island and Massachusetts, men like Patrick Henry, wanted each state to have its own militia. If each state had its own militia then no tyrant could use a large standing army to mistreat those not in positions of power in the government. Those notions were what brought about the second amendment to the Constitution of the United States.

So what happened with that part of the early experiments? Well there was a guy in Pennsylvania who wanted to make whiskey. He was damned good at it. He was so good at it that he made a lot of whiskey and began to sell it all over the country. Then the federal and state authorities thought he should pay some tax on the interstate commerce that he was conducting.

He said no and both the state and the federal government got involved in a small war over taxing whiskey. It was called the Whiskey Rebellion. So how then could the states or the federal government create revenue? Of course they taxed commerce just as had the British before them. In the ultimate the taxing power of the government, as near as I can tell, came down to having the power to enforce the taxation through the courts or through the use of force if need be. Hell the same thing happened with civil rights in the sixties. But somehow, after the involvement in the Vietnam War it became profitable to sell guns to the people of this country. Not just guns, though, but military weapons. So the NRA became a "gun lobby" that gathered so much power it could not be defeated. The wars after Vietnam, Desert Storm that popularized the military in the country like never before, and Bush's Iraq war and the Afghanistan thing brought even more military weapons to the public. It was really a Catch 22 for the State Police.

The first attempt at limiting military style weapons like AR-15 rifles and AK-47 soviet style rifles, so called "assault rifles" coming into the hands of the average citizen was passed by a Democratic Congress and then defeated by constant lobbying and the fact of a Republican Congress in both houses. In those times when that was happening I actually supported the end to the ban on military assault rifles. But the militia war changed my mind completely. I can tell you we had, in my dad's cave, over one hundred plus military style rifles, some silenced, most with flash hiding devices, almost all of which would fire one shot at a time, bursts of three to six rounds, or full automatic. We had a number of light machine guns that would fire bursts of six or more, as well as those that would fire only full automatic. But for the war, but for the idiots we took them from, I would have been happy to turn those weapons, all of them, in to the federal authorities. Why we did not I cannot tell you, except once again both dad and I discussed the possibility of more problems. Our conservative outlook had nothing to do with politics. It had to do with the ability to defend our family if the need arose once again.

You give a guy a pistol, his age makes no difference, his race or culture makes no difference, and all of a sudden he is John Wayne. You give a military rifle to a young guy and he becomes a soldier in his mind, a legend in his mind as well. Give him a weapon that fires full automatic and it almost creates an erection of his penis just thinking about firing that thing. Here is something I read back in the period of about 2010. I was shocked by this one. In one year about 120,000 pistols were left laying on the ground at *crime scenes*. No wonder there were so many murders in Frenchtown.

Weapons are purposeful tools for me, for my dad. We used them in the war in Vietnam and Afghanistan for their designed purpose. We used them to kill other human beings. That is what they are designed for, it is their only real purpose to exist. The militiamen used them for the same purpose. Then we turned our skills loose on those fools. Is there a difference between us and the militias? Qualitatively I constantly argue with myself there is but I cannot define it very well. My equivocation has to do with the unfortunate killing we had to do.

We used these weapons to defend our society, our home, our family and the families of others. They used them to steal, to murder without any restraint or reasonable basis for their actions. Does our way of using the weapons justify everything we did? Hell I don't know. I will leave it to God to decide that issue.

One thing I do know and that is the guns we faced in Frenchtown and in the forests surrounding our little town, should never have been in the hands of those who had them. Here is the final arbiter in regard to this reassessment of what we did. Had those in the militia had no guns, civil authority could have been maintained and the murders which occurred would never have happened, at least it is more probable than not.

The murders that were committed, the atrocities inflicted by those in the militia we defeated were in the thousands. There were so many new graves in Frenchtown they could hardly be counted, and some of the dead had just been thrown into the forest. No one knew who they were and no one wanted to dig them up and find out. There were horrors associated with seeing those people mutilated as they were. Atrocities are not pleasant for anyone. I have done an inadequate job of describing the atrocities to you. Suffice it to say I will likely have bad dreams about them all the rest of my days. There is no justification for wanton killing. I do not justify myself or my Dad for what we did. What the militia did was another kind of killing though. The faces of the children haunt me.

The only thing we really had to do after eliminating the Army of Northern Idaho was to wait. But we did have to try and help the city people, some of whom had no experience or knowledge of how to operate a water system, for example. The water had been shut off because electric power was gone. Power was still a problem. But water could be provided by the gasoline powered generators operating the pumps for at least a few hours a day. It would enable the people to go to the homes they had fled. When and if they came back after the war and found their homes boarded up they would be able to reestablish themselves in a house, whether theirs or another, at the very least. The use of power to move water made possible the operation of the sewage systems again as well. Funny, until the sewage systems were not operable at all I never thought about them much.

Power would also enable the State Police Barracks to operate again and it did so. The State Police eventually were able to bring in their own electric generator to have full electric power the day around. Power enabled them to get their radio systems operable and then they could begin to patrol the highways again. But then they had to start hiring people to operate the emergency systems, jobs began to open in the governmental systems again and people began to go back to work. Many of the people, like the Powers families who had occupied three homes in Frenchtown, were all dead. Some of those who came back just moved into the homes that had belonged to the Powers family and began to live there as though they owned them. Title to real property had broken down completely under the militiamen. They were not concerned with ownership of anything except the stuff they were stealing from those they were raping and murdering. No one really cared about deeds of titles to cars after the war was over.

The cars which had been drained of as much gasoline as the militiamen could get out of them for their trucks were taken by some of the new people that came in, and some of the old people that came back. They occupied homes they had once lived in if they could. If they could not they took homes of others who were dead and gone. If there were televisions, stereos, entertainment tools there which had belonged to someone at some point in time, well now they belonged to the people who were new, who were squatting on the property. No one argued. No one fought over which house belonged to what person.

Most of the militia people had been in their twenties and thirties. Most of those in the forties and older age ranges were encouraged by the younger ones to get the hell out of town. Many in those age groups were simply shot to death for no reason. Some of them made it down to Missoula without managing to see a policeman and lived with relatives or simply moved on to parts unknown and by means unknown as well.

Some of them had homes in Frenchtown and wanted to come back. Some did return. Some took up residence as they had before the militia. Some of those who returned began to operate restaurants and motels and businesses of one kind or another. There was not much going on business wise but what little there was had people there to handle it within a month.

"AFTER THE MILITIA." It was the name we came to call those times. We were a little premature but we didn't realize it then. As things settled down life returned as much to normal for all of us as it could. For all of us at the Rancho de Young normal was a little different than elsewhere perhaps. We hunted, continued the processes of refining our defenses, helped our ladies with growing a few different kinds of produce. We were able to get several of the hanging tomato planters and they bore fruit very quickly. We centered on us and helped others as we could.

Chapter 10

What is Going On In the World?

The question was always on our mind. All this had started so innocently or so it seemed. In fact, I am sure there were a number of people who wanted nuclear war. Those of the faith of Islam who thought it would enable them to establish a world wide Caliphate found what it did was take their countries nearly back to the stone ages with a few notable exceptions. And boy did those begin to take control fast. The Saudi Royal family moved into Iraq, Syria and Lebanon post haste and established control over the small remaining populations in those countries as quickly as they could.

Baghdad no longer existed as anything except a constantly flaming pit of stinking burned up flesh. The same was true of Tikrit and several other Sunni cities in the western part of Iraq. The two major cities of Iran, Teheran and Qum, were much like Baghdad. New Delhi, many of the eastern and central cities of India, Islamabad and many other cities in Pakistan had simply disappeared in the ash and blast of powerful nuclear weapons. Many of the parts of Pakistan and India which had been hit by nuclear weapons were still burning over a year later.

In Lebanon, in Syria, in the Crimea, in parts of Ukraine, in much of the central part of Russia there were burned out hulks of what had once been cities. D.C. was gone. Almost all of New York was gone. Much of Miami and the central part of Florida had been bombed and shelled so badly that it was a series of holes, sinkholes and pock marked terrain. The bombings had taken place as the Cubans tried to advance up the Florida peninsula and were eventually handed their asses.

The Cubans had been pushed back from advancing as far north as just below Atlanta. From there to the south in the U.S. was a mess. Much of the center of Nebraska was on fire. Much of northeastern Montana, western North Dakota and South Dakota was still on fire many, many months after the nuclear explosions ended.

The North Koreans had been reduced to an army of men armed with rifles and artillery but little else. They decided when told by the Chinese to do so they would stay out of any further conflagration. There was little else they could do. Their nuclear capability had been destroyed, their Air Force had been shot to pieces and their air fields bombed so badly whether they could ever be used again was an open question. Their vaunted submarine force sat on the bottom of the Sea of China.

Formosa had received some bombing with standard weapons but all the damage had been repaired within hours. The U.S. Fleet in the South China Seas were no longer under threat by the Chinese. The problem for the U.S. Fleets around the world, those which were still at sea, was no civilian command structure existed right after the war. So they relied on their military leaders. In some areas of the world that is how the nuclear exchange continued. Iran was decimated by

Israel. But it also hit the Israelis. Syria tried to do the same and was obliterated by American planes from the U.S. Fleet.

The Japanese were firmly in control of their people and Japan was still cranking out everything in its economy it had been producing before. They just had to find different markets to plumb for a time. The markets would not be a problem. The Australians, who had not been involved at all, wanted their products and those of the Chinese. So did the Malaysians and the Indonesians who had not been marked by the war. South America and Central America as well as Mexico were ripe for the products of the Far East and trade pacts were quickly authored with all those areas and countries by the Japanese and the Chinese. So apparently world wide trade was resuming without the booming/busting economy of the United States.

Most of the information we got came from Radio USA but occasionally we caught a television program out of Portland or Seattle. There were many problems with the microwave towers which had, prior to the nuclear exchanges, operated with such efficiency. The Electro Magnetic Pulse damage caused by the nuclear explosions was not limited to earth. A lot of satellites were damaged as well. Some were shot down deliberately by our anti missile defense system. The loss of satellites made it impossible for anyone to steer their nuclear missiles except by inertial programming and that could be off by hundreds of miles. That was how New York got hit. The unit that exploded over New York had been meant for D.C. along with the other seven units in the warhead. Six of those other seven from the missile which hit New York got shot down. The other one got D.C. The explosions in New York and D.C. were monstrous.

So New York was out and the hub of the world wide stock exchange system had been destroyed. But then so had London, so had Moscow, so had Paris. That left China and Japan with the only viable stock exchanges in the world having world wide capabilities. But they had no frame of reference any longer. The dollar, as the world's monetary standard, was gone. There was no way to measure its worth.

All the equities so treasured by "investors" had been destroyed in the banks which had for all intents and purposes been melted when New York was destroyed by at least a twenty-five megaton thermonuclear warhead. No, not every building was completely rendered useless or even badly damaged. Some on the fringes of the city remained viable. Manhattan, Long Island, all the buildings there, the center of New York, the diamond district, the entire financial area, no longer existed. It was simply vaporized for all intents and purposes.

Real property holdings of famous families were worthless. There was no one to value them because they either did not exist (example the New World Tower) or the family had been destroyed in their beautiful homes, condos, whatever in New York City and its environs. Many famous families had ceased to exist except for remote relatives. And what could they inherit?

Could they inherit a home on Lake Chautauqua? Most of those were ravaged and damaged severely by looters and militia types within the first week after the nuclear exchanges. Upstate New York still functioned fully but many places out in the forests of northern New York and eastern Pennsylvania were being attacked by criminal forces and those of anarchy. The western U.S. was not the only place filled with idiots with guns. Some of the idiots with guns were purposeful. Some were Neo Nazis. They wanted to create a New Order in our country. They tried to start doing so by occupying areas in remote parts of places like upstate New York.

National Guard units were brought together by their leaders where there was sufficient communication to be able to accomplish that task in the northeast. From the south came the urgent call to the defense of our borders. Many of the National Guardsmen, those who were younger and still possessed some sense of patriotism went south to be conscripted into the "federal" army which was fighting the Cubans.

What was left behind, the older men, even those who had some experience at jungle fighting and preserving one's life in the forest, were forced out of the towns right away. If they were lucky they made it to the cities like Buffalo where law enforcement was still intact though under siege by the criminals and the anarchists or Nazis.

We all waited. By all of us I mean everyone who was still living. We didn't know exactly what we were waiting for. The war in Florida was winding down. We had no idea how a new United States of America could form a government. The tunnels and underground installations in D.C. had been inadequate to the handling of a nuclear blast there. They collapsed and buried the President, the Vice President, the President of the Senate, the Speaker of the House of Representatives and virtually all the Secretaries of State and every other "cabinet" post under millions of tons of soil and concrete.

D.C. was not useful for anything after the nuclear strike. How did we proceed as a "government?" At first it would have to be with the military as our "ruling body" it appeared. Elections would be impossible. There were no cross country communication systems left save for I-10 in the south and west and I-40 through the west and mid-west. But telephone systems were gone. The companies which ran them had been centered out of New York.

Everything was in flux. Nothing was a certainty. So we waited, all of us, waited and waited for something to happen. And basically nothing did except time passed and the militias and anarchists got stronger.

At our "fortress" in the forest we made ourselves stronger than we had been before the war of the militiamen. We extended our listening and video capability in every direction. There was no way to approach the home area of half a mile or so in extent in every direction, without someone knowing you were coming.

We quieted and updated our generators in capacity and power output and built in more capacity to store fuels with which to operate those generators. Dad and I built conduits into the canyon in a number of places where the exhaust of the generator was disbursed with practically no signature of heat at all.

They would eliminate any heat blooms from appearing to a helicopter with an infrared search capability. The ends of those conduits directed the flow of the exhaust into buffers that spread the heat over several feet and there were many of them. It had been of concern to us in the first instance and we didn't want to be vulnerable if someone came looking for us another time.

We let the forest grow back over the animal trails, walked up to several miles to our vehicles if we went to the city, never walked the same pathways twice in order to avoid creating lines in the dirt that led to our home. We encouraged the forest denizens to come around, put out some salt for them in camouflaged pieces, put out some feed for them that looked just like the dirt they were walking in. And we began to bring as much storage capacity for food as we could build into the cave area into existence. Some of it was refrigerated. We packed as much frozen food into our storage as we could get or create.

The exhausting of those gases was through the same system as the generator. We brought in a lot of dehydrated foods and right after the war with the Frenchtown militias was over we went to Arlee and commandeered all the remaining MRE's which were available there. We policed up all the brass we could find wherever there had been fire fights in the forest or out on the highways. We started our own loading system with feeds and automated systems that made it a lot easier and faster to load new ammunition. Powders for loading bullets was hard to come by but we managed to get enough for thousands of rounds. We made our own bullets out of swaging systems and then dipped them in melted copper, allowing them to drip to a conical end on an appropriate metal sheet from which we salvaged and reheated the copper that came off those cooling new bullets. Waste not, want not was a mantra.

We maintained constant contact with the Montana State Patrol officers in our area and we tried to get news from the Idaho State Patrol as well. All of us knew that the panhandle area of Idaho had been a hotbed of militia groups before the war and probably was the center of any anarchist or militia movement if there was one left remaining after our war. We just hoped they would not come down I-90 and try and impose their particular brand of anarchism on our area. We tried to encourage some of our friends who had a military background to stay in the area, or in Missoula. We wanted their expertise and abilities if ever again there was a militia situation.

One of the things that we all waited for was some new kind of monetary system. But while we still had dollars and no way to know their value we were willing to do our trading, what could be done, using our currency. Things did get a little pricey though. There were good reasons for that. Only about two fuel trucks a week could get up I-15 to I-90 and across the mountains to Missoula. They would not try to go further than Missoula. Sometimes it was difficult for them to get through Utah.

But there was some commerce and most of it was done in dollars even if prices were a little dear. Gasoline was $100.00 a gallon when the truck had just left town. By the time the truck was back again to the stations that were given gas, those who could bear the cost of the purchase of the remaining gasoline would be charged upwards of $200.00 a gallon.

It was impossible to get such things as milk or eggs most of the time. A whole lot of farm products were unavailable in any of the market places. The farms in the southwest, California, Arizona, New Mexico, where they were not in areas controlled by the anarchists, could not produce enough food for themselves and everyone else as well. What they could sell and what little did get transported north was very dear in cost, indeed.

But some locals had chickens and it was possible sometimes to buy fresh eggs. And some locals, even in the Frenchtown area, had some dairy cattle and it was possible to get milk every now and again. Once again those things came dearly. But powdered eggs and milk were available and sometimes even plentiful. Everyone that was still around learned fairly quickly that it was not necessary to hoard things. The chicken cooperative did ease the problem of meat and eggs.

The ultimate bartering tool became ammunition. The .223 bullets that we were reloading and making ourselves were in hot demand among locals. So we could trade for milk and such things as honey, eggs, other forms of produce, and still maintain our large supply of ammunition. From time to time we also bartered a rifle. We only gave up those which were single shot AR-15's, and only to close friends and those we knew would not abuse having those kinds of weapons, for example our friends in the State Patrol.

One of our friends on the State Patrol, as it turned out, was Allan. We had no problem with trading anything to Allan. He was a true friend, a combat "compadre." He was a well-trained Recon Marine at one time before he left the Marine Corps. The Marine Corps was now a non-existent entity except for the structures and people that remained on a few bases. They were disciplined people who would not permit anarchists and militia types to take the armories or materials they held.

When Allan left the Marine Corps he became a State Police Officer. With the militia war there had been casualties among the "statie's" as well and the result was when we visited Allan in Missoula he was in charge of the barracks there. He was acting as a Major in rank in his police entity. It turned out, after we got to know him aside from fighting against the militiamen with him, he was very well educated, married and had three cute girls. His wife, named Karen, was a tall, beautiful woman that obviously loved him to death and vice versa. Our kinship of fighting the militia turned into a life long friendship. We always visited with the Coxey's when we went to Missoula.

We got together as often as our constant work on the home property and Alan's constant battles with militias elsewhere in Montana would permit us to do so. Karen and the kids even came out and stayed with us a couple of times. We taught Karen and the girls how to shoot a little better than what their dad had been able to take the time to ac-complish. And we taught them a healthy respect for weapons.

Allan had taught the girls well weapons were not toys nor exten-sions of their personalities. We taught them guns could and did kill things. We took them to the cemetery in Frenchtown to show them the graves of the unknown numbers and unknown people who had died there. Of course Allan approved and usually was with us when we did those things. His family became ours, ours became his in a very real sense.

It turned out we still had a governor of the State of Montana. And even though he had been too slow to call out the National Guard or too sympathetic to the anarchists he was still the governor for now. But the structure of the Guard, was gone. Most of its weapons had been stolen, most of its facilities had been so badly damaged or vandalized they were useless. The heavy weaponry which had existed in the armories of the National Guard centers in the State had been taken, as near as we could tell, to northeastern Idaho.

It appeared to us from all we heard (including information from Allan) a large and very well equipped army of militiamen had been formed in the area north of Coeur d' Alene. It also seemed likely that no one would challenge them as to their control of the area of the state of Idaho they occupied. So in respect to anarchists and militiamen we also waited, wondered, could not know what they were thinking or planning on doing. In many ways, though it certainly was a busy time, it was a time of great fears. So many things could still go wrong where we were, in terms of how safe our country was, in terms of the food and every day things we needed as supplies to use in our lives.

One really wonderful thing came out of the entire situation. My wife, my children, my parents and I all had the opportunity to reconnect, to spend a lot of time together and to learn how to survive as a family unit without strife. It was particularly great for my wife and I. We even took several small "vacations" together. One we took was amazing. As I said, the house that dad built was set with its back to a cliff. It didn't mean the cliff was not negotiable at all, just that it was a cliff.

Ruthie is not afraid of heights and neither am I so we rappelled to the bottom of the cliff, leaving our ropes in a position that would allow us to climb back up a few feet at a time while roped in to a strong point that would not fail.

There was a helicopter at the bottom of the cliff that had crashed there, due to my dad and I hitting it almost simultaneously with RPG grenades. We explored it a little. The human remains that were in the helicopter had long ago been recycled by Mother Earth. There were bones scattered around that the coyotes or bears, maybe even wolves, had gnawed at and left. The carrion birds had eaten their fill on these men as well. Other carrion which we had dumped over the cliffs from time to time were further away from the house. We left the area in which those remains were located alone.

The names of the pilots of the helicopter were forever forgotten. Their lives were forfeit for a cause which was not just. Neither of us wasted any sympathy on them. They would have killed us, both of us, after raping Ruthie repeatedly had they been given the chance. They even tried to kill our children. They were not given that chance. They were not worth our sympathy.

We found nothing in the parts of the helicopter that might be useful except a couple of boxes of fifty caliber ammunition. I tied the ammo boxes to a rope that my dad and my boys pulled up after calling them by radio and telling them what we had for them. Then Ruthie and I went off on a lark. We left the wreck and headed north up the little stream that was at the bottom of the canyon, away from the carnage of the helicopter crash and the many bodies further south.

We carried with us enough stuff to make a pretty nice camp. We had a tent and some soft bedrolls with fold-up cots we carried on our backpacks. We had plenty of water and purification pills for the water in the creek if we needed it. We planned to stay one or two nights. We ended up staying down there in the canyon for five days.

It was wonderful. It was loving, fun, almost like being college kids again, romping around half nude, or nude if we wished, reveling in each other. God, my wife is a gorgeous woman. I must have told her how beautiful she is at least a hundred times when we were in the canyon together. We touched a lot. We caressed a lot. We engaged in making love slowly and with great passion and speed, and we held each other tightly in the aftermath many times. We recaptured a lost moment of youth and sexual love as well as the deep abiding love we shared out of our mutual respect for each other.

I think it inspired my parents that we stayed down there for several days longer than expected, to reengage with each other as well. My kids, when we got back up the cliff said, "Gosh we are so glad you are back. Grandma and Grampa have been so mushy and lovey dovey since you left it was getting sickening." Ruthie and I smiled, said something like "It's good to be home," and then laughed with dad and mom like crazy about it after the kids went to bed.

One Friday night Allan came with his family for a visit, a chance for the kids to romp in the woods, and some decompression from the tasks of governing the Missoula area as well as the small communities near us. He was concerned about some of the things he was hearing from the north.

"We are hearing from our furthest barracks up Hwy 90 up near the Idaho border that the folks in Kellogg and the little towns outside the area are headed west into Spokane. They say Coeur d' Alene is getting pretty sparse in population as well. The militia causing problems there is concentrated in the Coeur d' Alene Forest to the north and west of the city of Coeur d' Alene, up in the Spirit Lake area where the FBI had its problems a few years ago."

"How well armed are they as far as your intelligence goes Allan," my dad asked?

"We think they may have some small artillery pieces, something like jeep mounted recoilless rifles, maybe even some mortars but we cannot confirm any of those weapons other than by hearing explosions. Its for sure we are hearing those and lots of them. So they have some kinds of artillery and plenty of ammo for them apparently."

"Where the hell would they have gotten artillery or mortars?" My dad was shaking his head when he asked the question.

Allan did the same and then said "We think they have been furnished by North Koreans and are being brought across the border from Canada after coming into Canada by ship from the Far East."

I asked, "Allan is there any indication they are coming our way?"

"Well yes, that is kind of why I wanted to come out here this weekend. We have heard that they are moving down Hwy. 90 toward us and their stated intention is to go as far as Missoula. They say they want to secure all of the eastern border of what is now Idaho. We have even heard crazy stuff like they are going to try and go northwest and occupy Seattle and all the coastal cities of Washington. They want to give themselves a port city from which to export goods. My friends," he said, "it's about to get crazy around here again."

Well that was a little bit of an exaggeration. It was quite a while before the militia from Idaho ever came close to Missoula. "I started thinking about this a long time ago. Dad; Allan, Ruthie, mom, kids, this is our home. We should not have to run away from our home. Those anarchists didn't cause us to run away the last time and they by God won't do it this time either. But," I said, "we might want to get the kids out of this area to somewhere a little safer than it might be here."

Then I turned to Allan and I asked him, "How many people do you have on the force now who are working Hwy. 90 or this part of Montana Allan?"

"Our roster expanded to twenty-four last week, Will. Why do you ask?"

"How many of those men have seen combat, do you know?"

"No, that was not one of the required answers on the application forms we were provided by Butte. But it would be easy enough for me to find out I suppose. I think a well educated guess based on conversations would be maybe fifteen out of that group."

"Do we have any other source of manpower we could draw upon and create a fighting force here Allan?"

"Butte has a National Guard outfit there. But hell, Will, those people don't have any officers who are combat experienced and worst of all they don't have any non-coms who are combat experienced. You know what has been going on here. Most of the eastern half of the state is a smoldering mass of jelly after the nuclear attack. The people at Montana University think we are damned lucky the attack didn't tip Yellowstone into erupting. It could have happened according to what I have been told and then it would have been Katie bar the door for us all."

"So the best fighting force we can come up with is maybe what twenty to thirty men? Is that what you are saying Allan?"

"I suppose so, Will. And I already know what your next question is and we have no estimate but think their numbers are over five hundred, maybe over one thousand. Of course with those numbers we would be talking about logistics, truck drivers, the whole nine yards.

They probably don't have one in fifty of their men who is trained as a night fighter in the forest, if they have any."

"As far as we know do they put out sentries every night?"

"Yes. You can see the lights of their fires from our planes flying out of Butte. We stay at least twenty to thirty miles away. They have fired some shoulder mounted SAMS at us when we tried to take a peek at them."

"And if I understand the terrain properly Allan there are three mountain passes of at least thirty-five hundred feet elevation for them to climb and go up and down and around curvy roads before they can get close to Missoula. What about their forest area? Is it like ours? More dense, or less so? What is it like up there in the Coeur d' Alene Forest?"

"You are sure right about the roads, Will, and the forest they live in is dense, more so than it is here. That is about all I can tell you about their place."

"Do you think it would be possible to slip one or two men in there in the dark, take some looks around, do a little havoc creation in their sentry posts, and slip back out again?"

"I suppose you and I could get in there in a State Patrol Cruiser, close in to the town, and do a little scouting, maybe have a little fun as well. Sure. But we would have to be out of there and back down this direction quite a ways by the early morning sunlight hours."

"Well all right then. We've got some fun to look forward to. So let's start getting our gear put together and pick the right guy so that we know he will have a place to go for about five to six hours before he comes back to pick us up. Silenced and bows would be good, and a very little food but a lot of ammo in already packed clips that are black as night and won't rattle. The old K-Bar is probably a good one to have as well."

"Okay, Will. I will pick my guy carefully. In fact I think I mentioned to you and your dad a long time ago that Marty Jimson was working with me. He will be our guy. He's another of our brand of war dogs, another Recon Marine. And I think he would relish the chance to go into the woods with you, Will, if you want to take him."

"I mean no disrespect to Marty at all, Allan. Having heard what my dad said about training him I am sure he would do well. But you and I have already been back to back once and our experience kind of makes it imperative for us to team again. So it will be you and I if our wives will let us go on this foray." I was looking at Ruthie when I said those words and she just laughed a little and muttered something about there being any chance of her stopping me.

It took us about three weeks to get everything together in terms of materials, timing for all three of us and our families, and preparation for the detection devices they might have selected to use to defend their enclaves. We had to acquire some ultra long range spotter scopes for this trip since we did not intend to go close to them at all this time.

Marty Jimson would do the driving and pick us up after two days of recon. He was going to go into Coeur d' Alene, the city, and stay there as though he was on days off from his patrol. He knew a girl that lived there and he was single and ready to get his ashes hauled so he was avid about the trip in a variety of ways. Marty is a good looking young guy, in his late thirties now, has some college education and wants more, but right now he is all about finding a willing lady who likes sex as much as he does.

Marty dropped us off about ten miles out of Coeur d' Alene at the peak of one of the hillsides that you climb coming out of the city. It is a beautiful place to be sure. It was full dark when we got out of the car. We headed right into the woods.

Walking in the Coeur d' Alene forest proved a little more difficult than it was in our area. The forest was denser, the canopy was less giving of moonlight, and there were no trails that we wanted to follow particularly, so it was very slow going. It was good for us to go slow. It took time to look for ground based devices which would pick up the footstep of a man if they were there. It also took a great deal of time to look constantly into the trees themselves to see any little tiny red dots that might mean a camera was focused on your dumb face. So we moved with great care and no speed.

We made some progress and were probably a mile into the forest by the time the dawn began to peek over the eastern sky. We found a deep, dark copse of trees and bushes, made sure it was not occupied by a bear or some other critter and moved into it for the day. As the forest lightened slightly we were able to gather some boughs of broken branches to use as the base for our bedding. We covered the little area we were in after making sure of drainage and set it up to drain away from us if it rained as it often does in those mountains. We made it as comfortable as it could be and created several small holes in our covered area by moving branches around gently so that we would have a view of the area in which we were staying. We went to sleep.

Our deal with each other was one of us would sleep until the other started to snore. Once snoring happened the sleeper would be awakened and have to stay awake and wait for the other one to snore. We hoped to make sure of no noise that way. Noise carries in the forest for a long distance. In the mid afternoon Allan woke me up. He had a finger to his lips and his weapon at the ready. I heard why in a matter of seconds. Someone, and they could have been fifty yards away or two hundred yards away, said "God dammit they have to be around this area somewhere. The seismic devices don't lie. They walked through here last night. Fan out a little more and we will make one more pass at it. Hell they may have gone out of here by now. Who knows?"

By the sounds of the group that "fanned out" from that conversation there had to be about ten of them. We sure as hell didn't want a fire-fight with that many and it was too light to shoot a couple and make our way back toward the road. They would just follow. So the only thing we could do was hunker down in complete silence and stay still and quiet, hoping they would not find us. After about an hour of hear-ing people thrashing around in the woods, mostly from a significant distance beyond our location we heard them gathering again.

They were all chattering. It was getting cold out there. There was a misty rain falling and the day was waning. The leader of this group said, "Okay, we will leave you, John, you Ray and you Nathan, to stand guard and watch the meter for movement. You have your radios so keep them on. If anything happens or these guys, whoever the hell they are wandering in our forest, happen to walk by just shoot them. Leave their bodies. The animals will take care of bodies after you have killed them."

What the hell? They were already killing innocent people? They didn't know whether we were a couple of teenagers who came out in the woods to get a little or what. They would just shoot us and leave our bodies for the animals to dispose of? That didn't sit well with either Allan or I. As the night began to fall we very silently broke our camp, packed up our stuff and moved out of the copse of trees, silently.

We could see their camp. They were only about fifty yards from where we were. They did not have night vision on. They were relying on light from the fire they set and from their flashlight mounted rifles to pin us down and kill us if they heard or saw us. They didn't hear us for sure. They were too busy talking and preparing dinner for them to know we were there. We ate the food they had prepared. It was pretty good but kind of too bad for them they didn't get to share any of it since they were all gone to another place.

Now we were in a quandary. If we moved around there would be more come to search for us. If we stayed put we were too badly out-numbered to fight and especially it was true in the daylight hours. Allan had his satellite phone. He called Marty and made arrangements for Marty to pick us up at a given milepost the next morning at or near six a.m. We decided to see if we could spot their seismic devices. We found a couple of them and disabled them. The results were astonishing. We had moved several hundred yards away from the two disabled sound detection devices when mortar shells fell exactly where those things were located. They must have them plotted by GPS. Allan and I both thought and remarked about the mortars at the same time. Then we very carefully got the hell out of there. We must not have tripped any other seismic devices because they didn't fire any more mortars at us. Or if we did trip other seismic devices, they saw we were leaving and let us go the way we had come. As the three of us drove back to Missoula in the early morning Allan said, "Those people are a little more sophisticated than those we took down in Frenchtown, Will. It is also evident they are a lot better armed and prepared to fight. I hope we have not stirred a sleeping bear up there. We would need a lot of people to stand this bunch off I think."

"One thing about them is for sure Allan. They are really defensive about their territory. But we have no signs yet of them wanting to add to what they already have."

For the first time Marty Jimson chipped in a comment about the group. "They are looking to expand, Will. Here, take a look at this. I found it in town while the lady and I were getting a bite to eat. These flyers are all over the place."

The flyer was rudimentary but to the point. It announced that the city of Coeur d' Alene was being annexed along with the city of Kellogg, into the "New State of Idaho and Washington" and soon they would expand westward and annex the city of Spokane, Washington. Marty added to the flyer's contents by telling us the lady had heard, in a loud bar conversation occurring earlier in the week, the talk was they would expand south as well. They intended to take over all the small cities and towns along the roads paralleling the national forests of the center of the state and they eventually intended to annex all the territory to the south as far as Boise. It appeared to mean they were probably going to try and take some land in Oregon and most likely toward us in Missoula area as well. Wow. These people were ambitious to say the least. Annexing most of Idaho could be a major task against National Guard, whatever.

The flyer had one more thing in it that was noteworthy and it was a warning to anyone who was not willing to fall under the authority of the government of the New State of Idaho. It told them to leave immediately. It announced the penalty for disobeying a lawful order of any official of the New State of Idaho or its armed forces. The penalty announced was death. No disagreement or argument would be brooked. The government was not a democracy, there was no vote to be had. If you didn't want to deal with them you had better leave.

To say reading these flyers was a little sobering is a gross understatement. We took them home with us of course. We wanted the people of Missoula, Frenchtown, all the surrounding small towns, to be aware of what the New State of Idaho people were planning, what their attitudes toward governing were going to be. There would be town hall meetings in our areas.

We were still trying to operate within the "democratic" framework of government even though it was tempered with the necessity for very tight law enforcement controls. The State Police force in Missoula was expanded a great deal by Allan. He took in some of the police from the old City of Missoula Police Department. He hired some from other small communities in the area which essentially did not exist any longer, like Frenchtown. He began to train them not only in police techniques but also in military style shooting and tactics of shoot, move, shoot, move, present no target to the enemy, conceal, shoot, move. He taught them all the stuff that we had used so effectively in the night against the Frenchtown/Arlee/Alberton groups. But his force was pitifully small by comparison to what appeared to be hundreds, if not thousands, of militiamen waiting in Coeur d' Alene to take over the entire State of Idaho. Maybe, maybe with some luck we could slow them, make them anticipate more losses than they wanted. Maybe we could make them decide the price for dictatorship of the State of Idaho was not worth paying. Dad and I discussed making them pay dearly, as did Allan and I. Dad, Ruthie, mom and the kids were safe in our enclave so long as the numbers didn't get too high against us. Even given a siege status, we could use new tunnels we had worked on all through the summer to our great advantage.

None of us thought these new "northern" militiamen, as we termed them, would do anything in our direction until the winter was over. Sometimes the snow in the mountains around Coeur d' Alene and between there and Missoula could be brutally deep, making travel of any kind except by helicopter or plane, extremely dangerous and difficult.

We were a little too sanguine in those beliefs I think in retrospect. Determination can overcome a lot of obstacles. This new group of militia people showed us determination very quickly.

Soon, late into the fall months, we began to see and hear small planes flying around the area of Frenchtown, heard reports of Arlee being a center of activity for small aircraft and Alberton as well, where there was a fine airport built just for that type of aircraft. A couple of times we saw a plane which seemed to be joyriding right down the canyon walls behind dad's place. By the time planes were flying our canyon we had done the best we could to camouflage all our trails, all our spider holes, all our sound powered or seismic powered listening devices and the small cameras that were concealed in the trees as far as a mile away from the house in every direction.

Then one fine snowy day we saw a group of men, ten of them, dressed in white cloaks, wearing snow shoes, slogging through the forest toward dad's place. They were all armed with the newest of M-4 rifles. Our television viewing devices and infrared viewing devices which were set out quite a ways from our house enabled us to see they were traveling in good military order. The went with a point man who was a quarter mile or so ahead of the main group. We could also see that each of them was equipped with sound powered microphones attached to epaulets on their shoulders and that each of them carried packs on their belts that indicated small radio devices for intercom between them.

They were not carrying heavy packs. This was a strong indication that they were a reconnaissance force, not an attack force. But they were also of a size that if they engaged successfully they could call in reinforcements very quickly. Since we had not heard anything from any of our compadres in Frenchtown we had to assume that either

Frenchtown had been occupied or that this group dropped into the forest from a helicopter or maybe even by parachute. They apparently dropped into an open area with maps telling them the direction they should proceed. Dad and I began to prepare to try and whittle them down silently. That would mean taking out the point man quickly and with complete surprise and silence so he would not radio back to his buddies. It would also mean concealment of the body for a time. It was very evident these people were not here to do us any good deeds so we acted accordingly.

The point man stayed separated far enough we were able to appear behind him from a spider hole and shoot him in the back of the head with no sound at all. We dragged the body into the spider hole, cleaned up the snowy area several yards back away from the hole and I stepped off several paces away from it in a different direction with the snow shoes. But we had no illusions. Our attempts at concealment were rudimentary at best. In the area where we killed this man we had some claymores which were very well concealed. We thought we might have to use them. We set a mined booby trap which would collapse the tunnel behind us and left it one behind with the point man. Soon we heard a large explosion and some dust filtered down the tunnel to us.

We looked with our computerized system at the cameras and saw some confusion amongst the remaining four who were standing. We set off two claymores and eliminated them. After we had made sure they were all deceased we stacked them up on a sled and dragged them into a defile that was filled with snow which when they were dumped would cover their bodies.

It was a stop gap measure at best but enabled us to clean up our killing zone and reset our defenses with no appearance left of anything untoward happening. But it was close. By the time we got done a Blackhawk swooped over the area looking for us and those ten men. We had policed up their weapons as usual. They each were carrying fifteen clips of ammunition. That is four hundred fifty rounds each. It was another indicator of the fact that they meant us nothing but harm. They had no food on them, nor camping gear of any kind, so we knew they came to kill us and then leave.

The clean up of the spider hole, digging out, taking out the body and reopening the tunnel was a chore but had to be done to maintain the integrity of our defensive system. The system had become three deep by the time this new threat appeared. The tunnels were disposable after being used for a killing ground but would need to be reopened each time they were sacrificed. It was easy to camouflage them in winter but not so easy when the snow melted. We worked from the tunnel end and the outer end knowing or having no expectations we would be attacked again that day. No one gave us any trouble.

After it seemed clear to do so and when our work on our defensive system was completed I called Allan on the satellite phone that he had arranged to get for me and asked him to have some of his people check on Frenchtown, Arlee and Alberton. When he called me back he told me it appeared that Alberton, some ten miles away, had been occupied by someone who had come in a group of Blackhawks and a couple of attack helicopters as well. The State Police Officer who had gone up toward Alberton had heard some traffic on his scanner indicating occupation.

He walked quite a ways to be able to do some surveillance and saw the helicopters and a smallish transport plane, something like a C-130 but not military, at the Alberton Airport. Frenchtown had not been occupied. There had been some air traffic over Missoula during the day however and one of his patrol officers thought they had seen an Apache or Cobra attack helicopter circling to the west of town along the highway.

We thought perhaps the troops we had encountered might have come from the highway as a result of Allan's report. We backtracked a ways in their tracks, walking backwards a lot, until we found their vehicle, a Humvee, with two more troops which we killed. They were parked near Charley and Berneice's home, concealed. They never heard us, or maybe they heard the arrows which struck their heads just before it occurred.

We took the Humvee, which was equipped with armor and a fifty caliber machine gun as well as a tow anti-tank missile launcher. It was of the style used on light troop carrying tanks of the U.S. Army, called Bradleys. It went back into Missoula. We left it with Allan who thought he had several guys that knew how to operate all the equipment in the Humvee.

It was getting late when we got home. We were able to make it to the most remote of our spider holes, one that was within a foot of the trail made by the militiamen, and use it to go on to the house. Nothing more had happened during the day but we felt assured the next morning or afternoon something was bound to happen again. We were right.

Once again it was a recon patrol through our forest, looking for us. Once again it was a group of men, this time twelve of them, two acting as point men with the other ten following at about a half mile behind. The two point men were separated by about a hundred yards from north to south and about a quarter mile from east to west toward the house. The entire group was moving very carefully and slowly and there was lots of radio chatter going on between them. They were using the same radio net as the men we had killed the prior day but a different frequency. We caught it on our scanner and dialed the radios we had to listen. This time to get both the point men, dad and I would have to separate.

Dad took off down one of the tunnels which would take him to a point behind the man nearest him and just in front of the body of ten other men. I went down a parallel tunnel which took me to a spot not ten feet from the second point man. I shot him and drug him into the spider hole, tried to clean up quickly and then heard a thud as the second point man went down.

Dad was forced to close up his hole quickly because at least one of the other ten heard the thud of the body and came running forward to find out what had happened. I listened as the rest of them discussed what they should do and where they should go. They had no clue that I was holding steady on three of them with an MP-5 ready to loose several quick bursts to kill at least three more.

Soon all of them were gathered round the area of the spider hole trying to figure out what the hell could have happened. Dad had gone to another parallel tunnel and called me. He asked quietly if I had a good angle to shoot. I said yes, he said on a count of three. We opened fire and at least six of them went down. I loosed two more claymores as all ten were in the kill zone. It was a slaughter. This time we took them down to Charley and Berneice's place to find another Humvee with another Tow Missile launcher and fifty caliber machine gun mounted on it. We loaded them into the Humvee and went to Missoula.

Allan and I drove the two Humvees with one man on the machine gun and two men each working the Tow missiles. When we got close enough to Alberton Airport to fire the Tow missiles we did so and destroyed the attack helicopter as well as one of the Blackhawks. We got the transport plane as well. We destroyed the other Blackhawk with the two fifty caliber "Ma Deuce" Machine Guns. There was a lot of firing back at us but it was apparent that they had not brought in mortars or artillery on this what they thought would be a short scouting and conquest campaign. The small plane which had been flying around our property looking for anything tried to take off in all this shooting and never had a chance when one of our guys lit him up with the fifty cal. There were not many of them left in a short time.

As their firing diminished we went closer and closer. They were inside two buildings by that point. We destroyed one of the buildings with the last of the six Tow missiles we had and began to cut the other to pieces systematically with the fifty caliber machine guns when a white flag was shown. We let the guy come out.

He asked for the opportunity to get the hell out of there with his few remaining men. There were five of them left. We had them disarm themselves as they came out of the building they had been in. We let them take a derelict car from the parking lot of the airport to go home in. We didn't know if it had enough gas or not. We really didn't care one way or another.

As they were getting into the car the leader said to us, "We will come back you know."

Allan said "It looks to me like you guys numbered about fifty when you came here. Five are going home and if we wanted you dead you would be dead. Does that sound like anything you want to go through again?"

"You can kill fifty of us. And fifty more will come. Plus many more than fifty more will come next time and they will have armor, artillery and more helicopters most likely. I won't be here. My men won't be here. You don't have to kill me. I was dead when we failed. My boss will do it for you. But he will know only four of you took this airport. And you will need one helluva lot more than four the next time, believe me when I tell you that." Having had his say the guy drove away.

Attack the Enemy when he is unprepared.
Appear where you are not expected.
Sun Tzu, The Art of War

Chapter 11

War Resumes For Real

At the start of World War II the Germans used their now infamous "blitzkrieg" tactics to overwhelm lesser forces or to outflank those which might be able to fight. They would then surround their enemy and whittle them down to defeat with bombing, massed artillery and ground forces, backed up by many tanks.

After the Germans had completed the conquest of Belgium, France, The Netherlands as well as annexed the Czech Republic, Romania and Hungary and taken Greece from the British, there came a period of quiet. This period of months on end without attack by the Germans anywhere became known in the press as the "Sitzkrieg." The press speculated the end of the war was at hand, said the Germans had accomplished all they wanted. Then Germany moved again and attacked the Soviet Union as well as conducting air war over England.

So it was with the militias of the New State of Idaho. The weather in our area, Missoula, throughout the mountains of Idaho, Montana, Washington and Oregon can be unpredictable to say the least. But in our spring, the first spring post nuclear war, we had a massive snow storm that lasted for about a week. After the storm came nothing for long enough for the forest to melt off, the creeks and rivers to run high and the ground to thaw, get mushy and then begin to firm up. Then they came. But this time we heard it was happening.

In the weeks before it started we made a lot of preparations to meet these people. We distributed a lot of weapons and ammunition to a lot of guys with some military experience who were willing to fight for their right to be free if nothing else. Our "force" mounted in size from around fifty to several hundred during the winter. And we trained, trained hard, ran, did all the work which would get ourselves and these new men and women in shape to be able to fight, move and fight again. We talked, we taught guerilla tactics, we taught them how to make IED's to attack tank or other forms of heavy and/or armored vehicles. And we "strategized" where those kinds of things could be best used.

And we begged for help from other sources, like the army. We communicated with what remained of the army units that had been stationed in California. At least we talked with those who had not been sent to Florida to fight the Cubans. We asked for "Special Forces" fighters if any were available. We sent dad on a mission to Camp Pendleton where there were still a few marines left. He made contact there without much promised help but did find a group of six more Recon Marines who put together their kits and followed dad back to Missoula as they could. They all arrived during winter at some point or another. When they arrived they promised the arrival of a van which came about a week behind them filled with Tow Missiles and launchers.

That was the one item we lacked so much until then, firepower, firepower strong enough to bring down a tank or a heavy armored vehicle like a Bradley fighting vehicle. And with these men came an abundance of Claymores which we could use in layered defenses to great advantage. We had no idea how many might try to attack us from this new group of militias, but we thought we had begun to prepare pretty well. From the marines we were also able to obtain some other significant weapons that we had not possessed in the past in sufficient numbers to withstand aerial attack. Those were shoulder mounted anti-aircraft missiles, fire and forget heat seekers that could bring down a spotter plane or a helicopter in one flash of explosive brilliance. With everything, and with planning which was pretty detailed about where and how to defend we began to be ready for whatever came. We started our first layer of defensive installations in Arlee and Alberton. Both these sites were somewhat mountainous and had curving or graded slopes which needed to be traversed by any force using the highway. Armored forces could not use the forests. There were too many large or small canyons, too many natural blockages in the forests. Still the forests could be used by men on foot. So we put out some seismic and sonic devices to warn those of us who would, in very small numbers, stay in Arlee when we heard the militias were coming, if we got the information. We didn't have to worry about knowing they were on their way. They sent planes overhead with propaganda leaflets which were dropped telling us to flee if we opposed them. They also said we could stand with them and face their enemies if we did not oppose them. They were so arrogant they even told us to the day when they would arrive.

This battle promised to be much larger and more ferocious than those in which Dad and I had engaged the stupid criminals who called themselves militiamen the previous year. When we attacked the group at Alberton Airport we saw they were dressed in military garb, carried themselves as though they were in good physical condition and acted with some precision indicating training and leadership of some capability. Facing a large group of people which was armed with artillery, mortars, aircraft and armored vehicles, was a completely different kind of task. It was a very daunting task indeed.

Since that was true we tried to get Ruthie and mom out of there, to send them somewhere safe. But where would that be in today's world was their question. Our little enclave, with all its tunnels and spider fighting holes, all its sophisticated and unsophisticated defensive tools was as safe as our world would give us. They stayed with us. It was not a surprise they did. Don't mess with Recon marines. They are bad people. But absolutely the last people you ever want to encounter in any kind of fight are the wives or Recon marines.

Ruthie and mom had to learn how to use some of these tools and did so to their credit. The same was true for my sons. God what a travesty to have to train children to use weapons against their fellow men, people they didn't even know. It simply had to be done. I had no illusions that my sons would be able to shoot a man. I knew that to protect her family my wife would do whatever was necessary including killing someone.

Dad and I were the early warning pair for Arlee. The NSI, we were calling them, came to Arlee in force but not their largest force. They had one helicopter circling around their column. The column consisted of a lot of cars, some modified and armored, most not, a couple of armored vehicles which resembled Humvees but were much larger, and a total of maybe two to three hundred individual troops.

The NSI came down the road in a column that was about a mile long with very little spacing between their vehicles. We had set some roadside IED's along that route as well as some in the center of the road and had one small bridge that wouldn't hinder them much ready to blow. It was behind them. We wanted them between us and a hard spot. It would make the attack we planned and executed much more devastating psychologically. When they had all passed over the bridge we blew it by a remote device from a cell phone. They stopped as we anticipated. We had several machine guns set up along the route which were also remotely operated a' la the Marine Corps' robotic devices.

They had small canisters which would empty quickly but which would create havoc and maybe some casualties. The number of casualties might depend on how many of the NSI came out of their cars when we blew the bridge. Almost all of them came out and pointed their weapons in various directions.

When we started firing the remote machine guns it was such a shock to those people they just stood still for a second. Probably thirty of them were killed or wounded in that first moment of chaos before they dropped to the ground and started firing in every direction. The helicopter also started firing into the forest, swinging in circles, firing machine guns and missiles toward whatever it was they were shooting at. Then it all went quiet. They began to assess their situation, remount their vehicles, look at the bridge behind them and move forward. The first of the IED's went off and blew up several of their cars which were bunched together. Car parts went flying in every direction along with some body parts. I don't know how many were killed or wounded in that first IED attack but it was several, maybe as many as ten. Again they fired off rounds into the forest in every direction. They brought out mortars and started firing mortars toward the areas from which the machine guns had fired at them, or at least what they assumed was the direction of the machine guns. They missed completely. Again they reassessed the situation, remounted their vehicles and began to creep forward.

The second set of bursts from the machine guns took some of them in their cars and some as they jumped out and started fighting again. This was all out chaos. It was exactly what we wanted them to think. If they knew two guys sitting in the forest operating remote devices were causing all this hell they would have turned and run backwards as fast as they could. They must have thought there were hundreds of us because they expended literally hundreds of rounds of ammunition each.

We couldn't know what was happening in Alberton but it was much the same as Arlee only on a larger scale. Our battle continued for a while longer and the machine guns ran out of ammo. We had explosive devices on them so that when the NSI found them, and they did, the guns would be disabled from firing ever again and maybe a couple more would be killed or wounded.

Wounds are just about the best to inflict in this kind of warfare. We had a few punji stakes set around the roadsides when the attacks first started. Some of them took a toll. The NSI people hurt by them would not fight again for a time. And some of those might die since we had made a paste from rat poisoning and put it on the sharp points of the stakes. These folks were getting the full bore guerilla war treatment. We would see how they withstood it.

These first games we were playing were just a start. We had two marksmen in strategic locations. As the NSI people dismounted and began shooting at nothing our snipers began picking them off, looking primarily for officers and non-coms, especially non-coms since we figured they would be the real leaders of this outfit. I don't know how many they took with their sniper's rifles but it was quite a number. After the second machine gun attack there were quite a number of bodies on the tarmac beside the cars of the NSI.

And so it went in Arlee and Alberton as well. We had layered in quite a few IED's. As the NSI advanced toward or into the towns they paid, they paid for every inch of road they took. And they paid with wounded and killed at every turn of the road, at every slope of the road, at every flat spot. The second IED attack was on one of the armored vehicles that had taken the lead at that point and had separated itself from the column by a good two or three hundred yards.

As it came forward around what was essentially a blind corner for its occupants we let loose an IED that consisted of about ten pounds of explosives packed under about five pounds of steel pieces of one kind or another. Those in the vehicle had little chance. It was destroyed as they were, without a fight, without us having to do anything but for pressing a button and unleashing hell. A large number of their troops, at least thirty or forty of them came running up toward the armored vehicle to see what had happened. We cut down about half of them with Claymores that had been placed in the trees alongside the road and were in downward or enfilade fire on the men that came under them. Many of those that were not killed by the claymores were wounded.

I guess they must have thought they would take some casualties because they brought a number of ambulances with them. Those had filled up with casualties in the first two attacks. These new casualties were loaded onto stretchers and thrown in the back of large trucks which disgorged more men to throw into what they thought was a firefight. It was not a fair fight at all. We got both their armored vehicles. One of our snipers was also great with a shoulder mounted SAM and he shot down the helicopter. The two snipers, while the NSI people were firing blindly at trees, were shooting more and more of their troops. Dad and I joined in that effort as well while being mindful it was our lot to operate the IED's primarily. Did I say that they brought two or three hundred people in that column? By the time they had reached the first exit into Arlee off the highway more than half of those people were wounded or dead and they had lost their helicopter and one of their two armored vehicles.

Some of the force of the NSI started down the ramp into Arlee. There were about twenty or thirty of them and it seemed likely they were going to make an aggressive move to find out who they were fighting. The first problem for them came in an additional set of claymores that we had placed on the ramps, all four of them, in anticipation of that move. The first set of claymores took out several and wounded more of the first twenty or so. More came along. The second set of claymores took out more. I guess they thought once the first set had fired that was all there were. They were wrong again.

Once more they were stalled, once more they were firing into the woods at nothing, and once more the snipers were picking off targets randomly. Another bunch of them died or were wounded there at what we called the off ramp battle. Again the same sort of thing was going on in Alberton. But in Alberton the force that came to fight was much larger.

Later, when Allan and I talked about the results of these battles he said there must have been at least five hundred of the NSI people coming down the hills into Alberton. They received the same kind of treatment those in Arlee were getting, none too friendly in general.

The next group of the NSI people that decided they were going to move into the town of Arlee decided that they would go down the side of the highway rather than down the off ramp. It was a smart move for them really. But we had anticipated that might occur and had placed some surprises there as well. They were called mines. The mine field was laid along the sides of the road for more than a mile actually and it consisted of the oldest mine used in the world though in the newer plastic version which our marine friends brought along with them. It is generally called a "Bouncing Betty."

The principal of operation of this mine is that it is tripped by a prong being stepped on or a trip wire, something along those lines. The mine then sends an explosive charge upward, which explodes at about six to ten feet above ground with a downward and outward effect. The "killing ground" for this mine is said to be about twenty to thirty meters in all directions. Of course we had put a lot of them out there, so when they started to be tripped, and then we set a few off remotely, there were more casualties amongst the NSI.

But a few of them made it into the buildings that were right next to the highway. We had thought they might try to do that also. We had mined or placed explosives in a number of those buildings. As they went into them we blew them up. Those that survived ran back up toward the highway with more mines taking another toll.

Apparently the few leaders they had left, and that was damn few I am sure, decided they needed to make a run for it out of town toward Alberton. So they all jumped back into their vehicles and away they went past the first of the destroyed armored vehicles, roaring up the street with the second armored vehicle leading the way and two cars hot on its heels. The next IED we set off was the equivalent of about one hundred pounds of explosive. All three of the vehicles were destroyed and all their occupants were killed. The second of the armored vehicles was the Bradley type fighting vehicle. It was surprisingly badly damaged by the explosion which lifted it into the air and turned it on its side. That was it. They were done for the day. The rest of them turned tail and ran like hell as fast as they could get by the destroyed bridge the hell out of Arlee and back toward the mountains of the Coeur d' Alene forest. We didn't really care how far they went as long it was out of sight so we could begin the clean up of this battle zone.

Most of these NSI people were equipped with the M-4 that could fire bursts of three, single shots or full automatic. Some had SAW's, some few were carrying long rifles the equivalent of a Remington 700 if not that same model. Most carried pistols and most of those were nine millimeter Beretta's or Glocks. We got one of the cars that had not been too badly damaged in all the fighting organized and started loading it with arms and ammunition. We took three Tow missiles from the Bradley and we found a few shoulder mounted SAMS in the cars that were littered with dead.

This was a massive killing zone. There were at least fifty to a hundred dead or dying in various poses around the road. Our snipers had really taken a toll. Many of the dead had one bullet hole in the head and that was their only injury. We loaded the dead into a large truck that was full of dead already. They were taken to the Arlee cemetery and buried in a common grave dug by a Caterpillar tractor.

The cars were pushed or driven off the road into the town, parked in various lots there and disabled after the gasoline was siphoned off into one of many drums we had stored in the town for that purpose. We didn't want this fight but whatever we could gain from it in weapons and/or the materials of war, gasoline for example, we would use.

We could hear the explosions from far away that meant the battle in Alberton was still going on. It was getting late in the day when we finished our tasks and headed down the road to the junction which would take us to our guys in the Alberton area. We, the four of us who had wreaked such havoc in Arlee, met up with our buddies outside

Alberton with some additional weapons, including some small sixty millimeter mortars, and more SAM's and Tow's. In addition we had confiscated several more fifty caliber machine guns that might come in handy along with a lot of ammunition for those guns.

When we got to our guys, Allan and six others, he gave us a report on the day's work. He told us they shot down the Apache helicopter at first light, got the first of two light tanks that turned out to be Bradley fighting vehicles, right away. After that the planned harassment devices they had installed, claymores, mines, remote mounted machine guns all had taken a toll. Allan estimated there were over five hundred in the initial push by the NSI forces. He thought that through the day they had killed or wounded at least twenty percent of that force. He too had snipers who shot their people while the NSI guys were firing off into the forest in every direction imaginable.

Allan said to me "A lot of their people are bottled up at the airport in pretty much the same places we attacked previously. We are too far away for their mortars or so it seems, but we want to go closer if we can. Do you think you and your guys can go closer and cause some havoc up there in the night?" I nodded.

I looked at my dad and the other two with a question mark in my eyes. All they said, almost in one voice was "Recon." We left and headed into the woods. We were back in our element, back in the "jungle" as it were, back where we were a lot better than anything the enemy had. We heard the first outposts within minutes. We killed them all within minutes later. The second layer of outposts were closer to the body of their force. We set up to take some of them out. We picked targets, used our bows and killed four of them almost exactly at the same time. Some of their buddies popped up to look and see where the attack was coming from. They died much as did their buddies.

We took off as quickly as we could expecting a mortar barrage to occur with parachute flares as the basis to try and discover where we were. It came just as we expected it would.

By the time the flares popped out we were on the opposite side of the road finding another set of outposts to raid. We took off another sizable number of their people in about two hours during the evening., Then worked our way back to Allan. From there the four of us went back to dad's place to get some rest before going back into Arlee in the early morning hours. We expected the remainder of the forces which had tried to come through Arlee to come back again the next day. They didn't disappoint us.

We didn't know how many they would bring again but it was about the same number as the previous day. This time they came much more cautiously though and without helicopters. Either they had lost all their helicopters or decided to use them for other purposes that were less dangerous.

The troops this time were walking in the forest. Again we had anticipated that might occur and in several places had set up mines and claymores in the forest on both sides of the road. Those items played havoc again with these militiamen. We killed a lot of their trained leadership the day before. This time we saw much rawer, less capable leadership, with its fruits being the loss of many more men. But this time we were a little more personally involved.

There were eight of us this time. Two of us were in the woods with machine guns which we had camouflaged and with which we once again devastated the troops of the NSI. They didn't understand shoot and move, shoot and move. We would fire around fifty rounds and then get out of dodge. We were camouflaged and blended with the forest so they had a hard time seeing us. We had pre-prepared firing parapets that protected us from return fire while we rained down enfilade on them. Once again they had no response or their response was ineffectual and scattered. Finally they got out of the woods and remained in the stance of firing in all directions, blindly wasting ammunition while this time four snipers took them out in wholesale numbers.

Again it was a slaughter. And the numbers of troops whose limbs were damaged or blown off were larger than the day before. The armored vehicles, as they came out of the Coeur d' Alene woods and into the clearing of what was Arlee were blown to pieces by both IED's and TOW missiles. The firefight lasted less time than the day before. Its intensity was lesser than the day before. The NSI was less avid this day about the battle.

This time though we watched them and harassed them with sniper fire as they retreated, causing more casualties. I think they went back at least twenty-five miles after the second battle in Arlee. We wondered how long they could withstand the losses they were suffering in this fight and the loss of weapons and ammunition as well as armored equipment and transport. We concluded they were not done yet and we were right.

The clean-up took longer than the firefight by far. We salvaged two more fifty caliber machine guns from Bradley fighting vehicles along with several more Tow missiles and this time the NSI left a truck full of eighty-one millimeter mortars and ammunition for our future usage. We buried those who had died, sent those who had not to the hospital in Missoula where they would be interned after their recovery from their wounds. We gathered as much ammunition as we could along with weapons and took them back to Missoula.

We went to the area where fighting had been renewed with the NSI outside Alberton and found our contingent of marines basking in a restful day after an early morning attack had been repulsed. Allan and I began to talk with dad about taking the offensive against the NSI people on the Arlee side. They were so schizo the second day and fearful of the IED's and mines that we felt it might be useful to show them an offensive capability. We decided that four of us, two of our buddies from San Diego and Allan and I would go up the road through the woods and see what we could accomplish. We drove part of the way and then did our woods routine. We sent two of us on either side of the road. Right away we took out two forward observation points and a roadblock which was occupied by kids who were less than fifteen. I went into their ring of fire and faced them up, four of them, with a buddy giving me cover.

One tried for a weapon. He died. The others began to cry and beg for their lives. I decided that rather than kill them I would break an arm or a leg on each of them.

I broke an arm all three and loaded them screaming in pain with their dead buddy into a pick-up truck and told them "If you want to live head for Seattle. Do not come back here again or you will most certainly be buried in Arlee before you reach the end of high school. You are facing men here. We will kill you. Look at your dead friend and know the truth of my words."

Hell I didn't want to kill kids. But I also didn't want to live under some dictator who would confiscate everything from me and then kill me, rape and murder my family as he had promised in the flyers. Why these kids got involved I cannot know. If they went back to Coeur d' Alene their boss would kill them and if they came here again we would kill them. It made for quite a quandary for them.

We wondered if we hung around there for a little while what would happen. We set up a defensive perimeter complete with claymores and scattered a few mines with trip wires in the tree line areas next to the roadblock. We had already policed up all the ammo, guns and useful tools we could find amongst their dead.

A half an hour or so after the three boys left three pick-up trucks came roaring down the road firing out of their truck beds which were filled with men and firing a fifty caliber machine gun from each of the truck tops that was mounted on some kind of circular pod that allowed it to be traversed. They shot the hell out of the trees.

There were five of them in each truck. Four from each dismounted and began to look around. They were badly bunched up. Most of them fell when the first claymore went off. Two of the trucks were riddled with balls from the claymore and sat there smoking with a dead driver at the wheel.

To their credit three of the guys that were not wounded tried to get back to the fifties. They didn't make it. None of them made it. We policed up their ammo, dismounted the fifties quickly planted remote detonation grenades in each of the trucks and took off. We set off the grenades when we were about half a mile away and with satisfaction heard three separate explosions.

So we had made another small dent in their force and we had given them a reason to fear we might attack rather than just defend. Maybe it would suffice for a day or two, or not?

It did not. The next morning they came again only this time there was a force of about a hundred men who drove into the forest as far as they could and dismounted and moved through the forest from there to Arlee. Dad and I and our two assigned troops, Dan Marble and Jim Wooden, awakened early as usual, had breakfast, prepped for the day, armed and went into the tunnels for recon.

It didn't take long to see that we had trouble. The troops didn't appear to know where they were going but there were too many of them for just the four of us to kill or wound badly enough so they would be out of the fight.

Allan called on the sat phone about the time we regrouped at the house to discuss the situation. He said that a big push was being made out of Alberton toward Missoula and wanted to know what was going on with us. When I told him he said "Oh shit, these guys are better than I thought they were. They are trying to flank us from the direction of your place, put us in a pincers. Okay, time to put some of the reserves into the fight. I am going to bring up ten guys to set up a trap for the ones who are coming your way near Charley and Berneice's place. Let em come. We will hit them there hard, hard enough to drive them back to you. By that time you should have a trap ready to spring on them as well."

We talked about how to get all this done for a few minutes and then it was time for the four of us to set our trap for the remainder that would come back our way after they got hit at Charley's place. We had let them go on by without making any offensive moves. They didn't see our claymores or our spider holes. From those holes we could set up a grazing fire situation against them in some places, and from four directions at once. Soon we heard explosions and firing. And then it was quiet again for a time, more explosions and firing and a few stragglers who were wounded started to come back toward us. We took them down individually and quietly since the larger body of troops was behind them. The larger body had been nearly cut in half. They were not running but they were moving quickly away from the battle they had just faced. They were badly bunched up as usual. The first of the claymores took five by itself. We set off at least a dozen claymores. Most of the remainder of the force that had passed us by in the morning was destroyed by the power of the Claymores. But those who remained alive did not stay among the living for long.

From our place we sledded out some sixty bodies to Charley's place. There was a large truck waiting there to take them to the Missoula burying ground that was getting heavily populated. The four of us then turned with about twenty of our trainees from town toward Alberton to go and help our buddies.

When we got close enough to the Alberton battleground to see what was happening it was clear our guys had held and were pounding a force which was at the airport in Alberton. We decided to pound them badly. We began dropping sixty and eighty-one millimeter mortars on their evident positions. It was not long before we once again saw a white flag. Allan and I were designated to get close enough to talk. We took an angle through the forest that put us about three hundred yards away and called them on the radio on their principal frequency.

The radio crackled and a voice came on saying "This is General Wayne Halloran. I am in command of the forces you see arrayed before you in Alberton as well as those occupying Arlee by now. Are you prepared to discuss the terms of your surrender to me at this point in time?"

It was about as arrogant a piece of military bullshit as I had ever seen. I said to him in return, "General Halloran, the only area your force in Arlee is occupying is the graveyard that is getting full in Missoula. Here are our terms for surrender, which would be your unconditional surrender of all your forces, General." From a second radio we had on our own net I ordered ten mortar shells to be dropped on top of them. Our boys were getting quite accurate with those things. We saw several bodies fly into the air and after the smoke and fire cleared or was put out the radio came on again. "Do you mean to suggest to me that our force in Arlee has been eliminated?"

"To a man," I replied. "Would you like another demonstration of our terms for your immediate surrender of all your troops and equipment, General?"

"Where would you like those of us who remain to gather?"

"Just outside the main area of the airport there is an area that is fully lighted with large lamps. Do you know where it is, General?"

"Yes, yes I know where it is."

"You will march your men in good order and appropriate ranks to the area, General. There will be a large truck waiting there for you. Into that truck you will deposit every rifle, missile, mortar, pistol and all ammunition for the same. No man in your unit will keep even so much as a K-bar. Do you understand quite clearly, General?"

"Yes, I understand."

"You have ten minutes to start your march, sir. On the exact moment of the eleventh minute you will be attacked again. Is that clear?"

"May we keep our clothing, our uniforms?"

"When you arrive and have deposited all your arms and ammunition in the truck which will be provided you will strip your uniforms and drop them on the ground. When they have been cleared away and burned you will be provided with some civilian clothing that will enable you to survive long enough to get back to Couer d' Alene if you wish to go there. If you choose you may walk toward the Oregon border instead. But that will be after we have had a little conversation, sir. Are all these terms clear to you?"

"Yes, yes it is quite clear."

"Here is a little something to think about while you are completing the requirements we have just given you, sir." At that point one of our snipers in the tree line near us took the General's helmet off with a thirty caliber round. He didn't hit the General, just the helmet the General wore. I said to him after his helmet was gone, "You are not a soldier, sir. You are a civilian. You will not put the helmet back on your head again. If you do the next round will go between your eyes. Get with it Mr. Halloran."

Halloran gathered what was left of his force in the area we had designated within the allotted time and they were damned fast about getting their weapons loaded in our truck and their clothes off them and in a pile. Once they were done we had some of our people go down, move them to a hangar facility where they would be given civilian clothing and sent on their way on foot. There were slightly less than one hundred of them that we dressed. Halloran was brought during this process to a private office where Allan and I awaited.

"Sit down Mr. Halloran," Allan told him. "We have some questions for you. And you will answer our questions Mr. Halloran. If you do not you will simply be executed. Am I clear enough?"

"Yes. What do you want to know?"

"First of all, how many troops did you commit to the attacks along these roads through Arlee and Alberton, sir?"

"Just under one thousand actually. We had a total of four Bradley fighting units and/or another form of armored vehicle that we committed to Arlee along with several armored Humvees."

"We want to take the opportunity here to thank you for the armored Humvees Mr. Halloran. We captured all save for one. It simply had too much damage to be useful. But our motor pool people are cannibalizing it as we speak so we will have spare parts for those we are now using. Another thing we need to thank you for is the usage of your mortars. Both the mortar companies you sent down here booked it when they started dying. We have all of that gear now as well."

"So we noticed when you were raining mortar shells on us a little while ago. How do I refer to you, sir? Are you the commander of the defenders of this area? Who the hell are you people anyway? You have knocked out the finest units we have trained in the past years. Are you some kind of charlatans or what?"

"You may call me Allan, Mr. Halloran. That will be sufficient information about me. You have no need to know anything else. But thanks so much for the compliments on the outcome of this little three day war. But now Mr. Halloran I would like to know if you plan on going back to Coeur d' Alene or heading south?"

"I will have to head south," he said. Then he added "If ever I saw the leader of the NSI again he would have me shot. He does not brook failure. His name is Cecil Fordner. He is an ex-CPA who had been involved in the militia for a long time. When the nuclear war came he had a plan. He murdered all his rival leaders and took over the entire encampment within forty-eight hours. I would not be surprised if he is coming here to Alberton tonight, in fact. He often visits the"war" zones to see how his troops are doing."

"So how many of you do we have to kill before this stops?"

"How many of us have you killed already?"

"Look guy you say you came down here with a thousand troops and less than a hundred are going home. Do the math for yourself."

"Where the hell did you get all those claymore mines?"

"That my friend is none of your business. But we need to know if your 'leader' is going to send more troops down here and if so with what equipment and in what numbers?"

"Of this you maybe be sure Mr. Allan," Halloran replied, "there are many more troops available to him. And he is most likely going to keep sending them this direction. He has a strategy. His strategy necessitates his controlling his eastern flank. You are his eastern flank. Therefore you must be under his control. If you are not he will continue to attack until you are. It's very simple really."

"What kinds of equipment does this guy have other than the Bradley's we have already destroyed? Does he have any heavy tanks?"

"Not that I am aware of. But remember he is working toward the west as well as the east. His push, when we started here was to solidify this flank and then attack and take Spokane. Once he had Spokane and this flank was not exposed he could go south to Boise. So you are in the cutting edge of his plans. So far he has committed over one thousand troops down here. I think he has another two or maybe three thousand in his command. There are more Bradley fighting vehicles and there are more heavily armored and armed Humvees. Since you have eliminated the forces on the Arlee side I would guess a heavier push will come through Arlee until the boys from this side make it back to his lines. His forces would be about thirty miles west of Alberton. When it will happen I cannot tell you."

"Okay Halloran. Walk. Take off. Go south, go west, go whatever direction you wish but do not ever show your face in this area again. If you do you will find an early grave." Halloran left, headed toward Missoula. He would be escorted through town when he got there. He had about thirty men with him. The rest of them headed east. We gathered all their weapons and ammunition, including what was left of the mortars.

We took the two badly damaged Bradley fighting vehicles onto a flat bed truck and hauled them back to Missoula where they would be parted out or maybe an attempt to repair one of them might take place. We already had a lot of parts for the Bradley and weapons to mount on any we could make serviceable. Actually if we could find a way to use the thirty-seven millimeter guns they mounted it would give us some additional stronger firepower. The guys in Missoula would be working twenty-four hours a day to try and achieve that purpose.

Dad, Dan, Jim and I headed back to our "fortress." We would not be able to stay long. There were preparations to be made. But we needed to rest, recharge our batteries with some good home cooking and make contact with some people other than those we were killing or who were trying to kill us. The battles of the "militia" wars had been fought for nearly a year. The warfare was beginning to take a toll on our minds.

We got home to find the kids playing outside for a change. We had been able to cannibalize some radar from one of the Bradley fighting vehicles which gave us a little warning about planes or helicopters in the area. The women had become very proficient in its operation. Dan and Jim played with the kids for a time to give dad and I time to reconnect with our wives for a moment. Neither of them were married though both had been at one time or another in their careers as Marine Corps Recon fighters. We hoped to be able to convince them to stay in the area when the fighting was over. There were a lot of single women there now and not many eligible men. But there were no guarantees for any of us life would continue. We had to anticipate, deal with the learning power of the enemy and set new kinds of traps.

Chapter 12

Assault, Run, Assault, Run, It Becomes a Way of Life

Dad always was thinking of new ways to create traps for the NSI. He came up with a really interesting idea we decided to follow up on. Just outside the woods, not more than a hundred yards or so away from a forest so dense it was difficult to see into its body in daylight, we dug some trenches about fifteen feet wide and about fifteen feet deep. These were not for personnel particularly but would be if they were stupid enough to get into them. And in the bottom we set punji stakes of course but also anti-tank mines and anti-personnel mines as well. The mines could be exploded remotely or by contact.

It took us the better part of two days to complete the trenches and to put lattice works over them that would hold enough flora and forest trash to make them look like they were the same as the rest of the ground around them. We placed these trenches about two hundred yards away from the on/off ramps for Arlee. Our thoughts were if the NSI people might avoid the road completely this time and crash through the forest. So we set some claymores to get their attention at the edge of the forest. We wanted those devices to drive them further into the forest and line them up with the trenches.

We expected them to lead with their armor this time. And they did, coming right through the forest as we had hoped, right straight at the traps. We had placed some IED's along side the road as well. We caught some of their troops in the open areas on the edge of the forest, popped some claymores at them that drove them deeper into the forest and onward they came. It was hard to tell how many they were this time because most were in the forest. Those we saw on the road were in pick-ups with fifties mounted on their tops, firing indiscriminately in every direction. They actually fired within ten feet of the four of us at one point. We watched them with high powered spotter scopes and glasses. Dan and Jim were once again our snipers. We equipped them both with fifty caliber rifles and regular Remington 700's this time so they could shoot at a little longer distance.

As the pick-up trucks began to come toward the town, down the highway, four Bradley fighting vehicles broke through the trees almost simultaneously. Dan and Jim had been playing with the trucks, killing their gunners and then shooting the drivers. Two of the pick-ups lay on their sides, on fire. Around them were scattered a number of injured and dead. None of them would fight anywhere ever again. The rest of the trucks, and we could hear more, stayed out of sight further behind those which had been destroyed already.

The Bradley fighting vehicles fired their thirty-seven millimeter cannon into the town for a few minutes, looked things over and being on what appeared to be flat ground that could be covered quickly they kicked off toward us at a high rate of speed with a large body of troops following. The four pieces of armor hit the ditch at the same time and went in fast and head first. It looked to me as though when they went in they likely stuck their noses in a downward trajectory into the bottom of the ditch or maybe the wall opposite of their entry points. Maybe fifty troops spilled in after them. We fired off the anti-tank mines we had placed in the ditch as well as some claymores that had been in the wall of the ditch. Nothing came out. Not many men came out. Those that did we shot with our sniper rifles.

There were fires burning below quite evidently and we began to hear ammunition cook off. We had placed some charges into the slope they buried into. We let them off and buried the Bradley fighting vehicles under an avalanche of dirt. That must have really pissed off the main body of the assault force which came roaring down the road firing in every direction.

Jim and Dan killed several of the drivers with their fifty caliber rifles. That caused a couple of wrecks that left many laying around again. We started mopping them up one at a time. We meant to leave them with no troops left to fight one way or another. We figured that if we killed enough of those bastards the rest would either desert their dictatorial leader or would refuse to fight us again.

But the main body this time was a large body of troops. There were probably at least three to four hundred of them. Later we heard another five hundred tried to attack Allan and his forces on the other side near Alberton. So they had thrown another one thousand lives to the wolves with no results again. As the large body of the troops broke out of the woods and came down the roads we ate them up with automatic weapons fire from fifty caliber machine guns, light automatic weapons and SAW's. There were no more than fifty of them still firing at us when they began to run back toward the west. I don't think any of them ever saw us or figured out where we were located so they could try to drop mortars or artillery on us. But they did shell the town of Arlee after this battle was over. They shelled it for an hour or more and then it grew quiet again. I think they were waiting to see what we would do.

We did nothing. We watched, we waited, we stayed under cover of the forest, in our prepared positions that overlooked the Arlee valley. After an hour or so of shelling they apparently decided to send out some patrols. There were three patrols that we saw. I don't think there were any others. Each of the patrols had five men in them and they looked to be better at moving in the forest than any we had seen before.

We let them go into town. There was nothing there to benefit them save for some buildings that they might want to try and use to house troops or equipment. Apparently they decided we had gone. They did not come into the forest on the south side of town where we waited. Hell I don't think they had a clue where we were. But one of the patrols did make an apparent attempt to flank us. We left Dan and Jim to deal with any potential from the ten that were now in town and went to the area closer to the highway where once again we had layered defenses.

It was getting near to dark when the five that had gone south along the west side of the road came out of the forest and started to cross the road. We took them in order as they cleared cover, last to first. They laid down and we policed their weapons and ammunition and went back to where Dan and Jim were having some fun, or at least it sounded as though they were having fun. When we approached their position we saw three more coming in a pincer type movement through the woods. They were less careful than their cohorts and paid a silently mortal price for their efforts. We took their weapons, went on back to where Dan and Jim were doing the same from a group of bodies just outside the tree line.

As I came out of the trees I said "Weren't you concerned about the other three?"

Dan smiled at me and said "Nah, we heard you coming. We knew you would take care of them. How many are there all totaled," he asked.

"I count fifteen more here but there is a mess in that ditch and beyond in the trees across the valley. I guess we will have to leave that until tomorrow though. But let's get these out of here into a house we can burn with them in it. Dad and I went back and got the others in the forest and out by the road, put them on a sled and took them with their brethren to a house that was pretty much useless. We burned it and a lot of loose lumber near it with the bodies inside, watched it for a moment after starting the fire and then went home for the night. No more of them came in the night. The next day they changed their tactics again.

The next day instead of separating their forces into two large units and attacking both Alberton and Arlee they came straight down the road into Arlee in massive numbers. There probably were at least eight hundred to a thousand of them when they started the attack. Of course we were somewhat ready for them and right away we discouraged them a great deal with IED's that tore up their armored Humvees. They had no more Bradley fighting vehicles apparently and no more of the large transport units that came out of the war in Afghanistan, the so-called MRAPS.

They lost a lot of men who were coming on behind the Humvees or alongside them. Losing men didn't stop them though. But their trucks began to falter and some ran off the road and turned over into minefields that then decimated the militiamen who were in the back of the trucks. Our sniping killed a lot of drivers as the fight continued.

Once again they had no idea where we were. Once again we hit them with claymores from different spots and angles than previously. And since there was no real strong force going at Alberton, Allan came with quite a few additional men that were extremely well armed and good shots. The NSI attack stalled, then was pushed back, then faltered and failed and they ran from the area back to their enclaves some fifty miles away. It was the last gasp of large bodied attacks we faced from NSI. They still existed. But their strength had been diminished so badly by our layered defenses and accurate fire into their ranks they were no long an effective large fighting force. I don't think they ever knew the small numbers of men they had faced. We were so lucky in all those battles. In the fog of war almost anything can and usually does happen, mostly negative. We kept them in the fog and we simply shot them to hell. Our plans thwarted their frontal attacks no matter how well organized. It was not just out of luck we all survived those attacks. It was also out of great planning and well prepared fighting locations.

After the last of the large scale battles the NSI began to send small units to our area to try and reconnoiter us. They came armed, they came with what appeared to be unfriendly intent. They left in the bed of a pick-up truck headed into Missoula and a common grave in an area filled with hundreds of dead NSI men and boys. After a time, I don't know, maybe they lost six or eight patrols, they stopped sending their men down to be killed. One day I was in Arlee working with the banker in an attempt to rebuild some of the infrastructure of the bank, the counters and the like, when a message came over one of their radios. We always kept one handy to make sure that we listened to their net just in case they should try to attack again. They were noisy buggers even on the radio. The message was short and addressed to "Allan." It said "Please meet me at the off ramp to the airport in Alberton on

Sunday afternoon at 2:00 p.m. I am Johnathan Corning. I am in charge of all NSI forces at the moment and would like to speak to you if I might. Thank you."

On Sunday Allan went to the ramp, or I should say went to the area of the ramp and waited to see what would happen. A single car drove up. There was one occupant. He parked at the bottom of the ramp, shut off his car engine, put the keys on top of the car, took off his coat, opened both sets of doors so that the interior of the car could be seen clearly from a distance, walked about ten paces from the car and stood there. Allan shrugged, looked at me and said "I'm gonna go talk with the man. I think that he really wants to talk."

We had positioned men in the edges of the forested areas and in any blind spots that might exist from the bottom of the ramp. Allan got into one of the Humvees that we had taken from the NSI and drove down toward the man. Allan got out of the Humvee, took his pistol off and laid it on the seat of the vehicle and walked toward the man. Allan had an open mic to a radio net we used so we could all hear the conversation or anything untoward which might happen in this situation. Nothing happened.

As Allan walked toward him Johnathan Corning took several steps in Allan's direction as well. He extended his hand and invited Allan to shake hands with him as he said, "Hi, I am Johnathan Corning. I have no military title but if you wish you can call me commander. I will be the last commander of the NSI forces. Our military enclave in the Coeur d' Alene has been closed. All of us who formerly worked with the NSI are now normal citizens of either the city of Coeur d' Alene or Spokane or one of the small towns nearby. And I take it you are the infamous 'Allan' about whom we heard so much from Mr. Halloran before Cecil Fordner shot him for treason."

"Yes, Mr. Corning, I am Allan. I was one of the people your army faced here in the Alberton area primarily but there were many others with me. And we operated in a great deal more democratic manner than your people did apparently. But you didn't come here to talk to me about our fighting capabilities did you?"

"On the contrary. It is exactly because of your fighting capabilities we are disbanding, leaving all our weapons in an armory that the Coeur d' Alene Police Department is taking charge of tomorrow, and going home to wherever that may be. There will be a few who will come to Missoula. Will your people greet them or push them away, I wonder?"

Allan and all of us in the area had taken vows at one point that we held dearly. When we were boys we were sworn into the Marine Corps. The vow of Honor, Duty, and Country never left any of us. Allan said, "Mr. Corning we are standing on ground that is part of the United States of America. This part of our wonderful country is the State of Montana. Where you have been privileged to live for some time now is the State of Idaho. Both those places are part of the United States of America. If your folks who come from Missoula are willing to swear to the State Police that they will protect and defend the United States of America and all its people we will welcome them with open arms. But if they are still living in this fantasy world you called New State of Idaho then they had better go a different direction."

Allan continued, saying "We, all of us who fought you here Mr. Corning, are U.S. citizens. Many of us are or were members of the U.S. Marine Corps. We love our country. She has been hurt. How badly hurt she is I don't know yet. But I do know that she is beginning to make a comeback. And part of her comeback was the losses you have suffered as a dictatorial militia group. There were others before you and others no doubt will follow in your rather unenviable footsteps. Those who do and who come afoul of the people of Missoula and the surrounding areas will no doubt be buried along with the more than one thousand of your troops that are interred outside Missoula presently. Does that answer your question fully Mr. Corning?"

"Yes it does Allan. But I hope we can be friends some day. I know you are wary, a little skittish that we might be using a ruse to prepare one last attack. Mr. Allan we have no guns left with which to fight. You are welcome to search my car and search me if you would like. And we would ask you to send a representative from your towns of Arlee and Alberton as well as Missoula to see that we are no longer a threat to anyone. In fact I would love it if you would come back with me today, share my home with my wife and children this evening and I will bring you back tomorrow. Could you do that, sir? It's not a long drive and I would enjoy talking more with you about your being a U.S. Marine."

"In a word Mr. Corning this conversation is a little strange to say the least. I could use other words as well. For the last month or so you have been trying to destroy me, trying to subjugate, rape and murder all those I love, and now you offer to have me share your home with you, your wife and children. I find this all a bit disconcerting and a whole lot strange. But, Mr. Corning, I will put the shoe on your foot instead. You go home, sir. You bring your wife and children to my home and you may share my accommodations for the night with my family if you wish. But I promise you, sir, if this is some kind of trick, some kind of device to get us to lower our defenses and our alert status you will be sorely disavowed of your trick and most likely be sent home in a body bag, if you are sent home at all."

Allan was adamant at that point as he continued, saying "Mr. Corning I tell you once more, and I will use an old phrase from a movie I saw long ago about the Vietnam War, you must understand that we are a lean, green, fighting machine. We are warriors. We were living peaceably and trying to put life back together again until you and your cohorts tried to kill us all. You have reaped what you have sown Mr. Corning. Can we be friends? Can two rattlesnakes be friends? I suppose so but the likelihood is not particularly high. Can I put aside from my mind all the dead, raped and murdered families the likes of you and your friends heaped into piles before we started to fight back? I suppose so but it is going to take me a while. And once more, while I am contemplating that if you and your friends think we will relax our vigilance because you came here you really are not very smart."

Allan had worn a police vest that day under his bulky coat. It was good that he did. He turned to walk away from Corning and a shot rang out. It hit Allan between the shoulder blades more or less. Corning stood there, shaking his head, saying to himself, "I told you this would not work." Allan stayed still. The sniper moved slightly and Dan acquired him and I scoped him. And Dan killed him. We went quickly to Allan's side and took him back into the woods. Corning was still standing there in the ramp area. He had on a radio and I tried their usual bandwidth. "Mr. Corning, come in."

He picked up his radio and said, "This is Corning."

I said "This is the last voice you will ever hear again unless within the next thirty seconds you get in your car and get hell out of here never, ever to return. Your sniper is dead. You soon will be if you do not leave. Do you understand?"

"Yes, yes I do and I am terribly sorry for this mess." He turned and walked to his car, drove away and true to his word we never saw him again. That is not to say they didn't come again. Was he with them? I don't know. If he was he died. All that came to us in small groups after the "ramp meeting" died, to a man. And finally in a little less than a year they stopped coming completely.

The end of the militia wars took place in 3 NE. We have shorthanded our calendar now and 3 NE means three years after the Nuclear Exchange. We ended it for good. We decided, after killing several hundred more of them in small skirmishes and ambushes such as those we used on the first militia group, it was time to get rid of their influence and ability to fight. We took three Bradley fighting vehicles and several trucks to the outskirts of Coeur d' Alene. We found the road to their main compound.

Dad and I, Dan and Jim, scouted ahead in the forest while Allan brought the column slowly forward toward their bastion. There were no patrols, no outposts, but there were seismic devices that we could see and a few cameras mounted in the trees. We disabled each in turn and moved forward. There was not much left of them. There were maybe fifty men. Most of them were not armed but for a pistol.

We gave them a chance. We announced on their radio we were coming and if they wished to surrender they should do so now. Some came out of the compound, waving white flags. I could see others running from one post to another inside the compound. Dan brought up the first Bradley and fired off maybe two hundred rounds into the compound with the large gun and another two hundred rounds or so with the fifty caliber machine gun mounted on the Bradley. By the time he had done that most of the buildings in the compound were on fire and a few men staggered out of them and fell on the ground.

Again we called on them to surrender. At first there was silence. Then as the second Bradley pulled into place alongside the first one they came out. They were holding their weapons of whatever type out away from their bodies. There were only ten left. We cuffed them and after collecting all their weapons and ammunition, as well as some food supplies and gasoline drums, we lit the place afire. It left a stain on the sky that lasted for a week I am told.

The stain of that particular group of murderers, rapists and would be dictators was done. The second of the militia wars was done. Thank God there were no more in our area.

We took the ten prisoners back to Missoula. Fordner was one of them. So was Corning. We tried them for treason against the United States of America and they were sentenced to life in prison with no benefit of parole in the once again working Montana State Prison at Deer Lodge. The others we sent packing in different directions with the clear indication if ever they showed their faces there again we would simply kill them.

Chapter 13

Life ANE (After Nuclear Exchange)

Post War

For three years after the nuclear exchange we struggled, we fought, we prevailed and we went on. But what did moving on mean? First let's take the banks. And this is in part a comment about how resilient Americans are. St. Louis, Missouri became the seat of the United States government. As near as we could tell from the television broadcasts we saw, and they were becoming more regular, everyone seemed to agree the gateway to the west was a good place to make a new start.

In each state the governor who was in power at the time of NE appointed a senator and held special elections for the House of Representatives to the U.S. government. The government began to meet, passed some emergency powers which were granted to the new president who was chosen by the new Congress. The new president is an expert in finances and would need help to rebuild the banking and insurance business in the country. Her name is Elizabeth Warren. The Vice President was also chosen by the Congress. He is from Chicago,

Illinois. His name is Rahm Emmanuel. He is said to be a real go getter, someone who can get things done in a hurry. Right away President Warren began the process of reestablishing the federal government. The army generals, navy admirals, all the military leaders that were left, were brought to the new "White House" in St. Louis and were required to swear allegiance to the new federal government of the United States of America. She also began the job of appointing new Justices to the Supreme Court of the United States as well as cabinet members. The federal government began to hire, was trying to reopen the post offices which had been shut since the nuclear exchange began. Many things were going on all at once.

We in Montana, Idaho, eastern Washington and Oregon were busy fighting the militia wars so we didn't get in on the process until a time after many of the other states. Many were not affected by NE at all. Most of the South, with the exception of Florida, parts of Georgia and Alabama, remained intact.

Part of Texas was gone because some Russian in Cuba got careless with a small nuclear warhead. His stupidity ended the city of Havana forever as well as the city of Houston. We, the United States, still had the most nuclear warheads stored of any country in the world. Cuba allowed a Russian to go nuts. We retaliated and that ended that. But you get the picture. It was chaotic in some places and others were quite the same as they had been BNE (before nuclear exchange).

But by three years after the exchange and with the end of the militia wars in the northwest we were beginning to find some normalcy. The fact there was a mint in Denver as well as one in San Francisco helped us in the west to get back on a monetary standard more easily. The banks began to receive credit in the larger cities like Coeur d' Alene and Missoula as time passed. That meant accounts could be opened and maintained, loans could be granted in smallish amounts, jobs opened in the branches of banks in our states as well as elsewhere.

Jobs were being created in very large numbers. A lot of infrastructure needed repair. A lot of work had to be done to begin the process of rebuilding an electric grid which was dependable. There was much to do to provide adequate food for everyone in our country and there were needs in the world in general which had to be filled as well. Trade with the southern states, the southwestern states and the South American and Central American countries as well as Mexico began to flourish once again.

One excellent byproduct of the exchange and all that followed was the ending of the American need for drugs from South America, Central America and Mexico. The reduction of the drug trade began to reduce the dependence of the poor people of Mexico especially on the cartels. Mexican labor was once again welcomed into the southwestern U.S. to help plant, grow and harvest crops, to herd and deal with cattle and other meat sources.

In general more people began to work at something, anything which would help, and as a result wages of some kind had to be paid. The banks borrowed money from the Fed which was renewed in St. Louis, the banks began to lend money to business people all over the heartland of America which was still habitable. Of course Omaha and its environs was excluded. A boom in employment and earnings began to occur and the boom made manufacturing begin to grow in the mid west again. Plants that had long been closed reopened. It was truly remarkable, almost miraculous, how the whole economy began to unfold as though the wars had never occurred and to rebound even more robustly without the billionaires who had begun to rule the country before the exchange.

Folks, don't get me wrong. There were many problems none of us seemed to be able to solve, but we learned, and eventually along came people who knew what to do. How, for example, do you operate a sewage disposal plant? Do you know how to operate a sewage disposal plant? Do you know anyone that knows how? Well that is what our cities were built to deal with. So how does a sewage disposal plant operate? We worked it out. There were people. They knew what to do. They took over and did the work.

How do you operate a water dispersal system? Especially in a place which has been bombed, mortared and has had claymores set off by the dozens? Did any of these explosions damage the water system that existed in each of the towns we fought over? How do you find all the mines, all the claymores, all the booby traps that you have set, much less those set by your erstwhile enemies in the militia wars? It had to be done. Some legs were lost, some hands and arms were severely damaged but the necessity prevailed and the job got done.

Doctors were really scarce in our areas. There were several in Missoula and an operating hospital there as well which had continued to operate even during the militia wars. Arlee had no doctors; the same was true in Alberton and Frenchtown. Some who had gone south into Utah came back to rejoin the efforts of us all to restore civil life to our states. Births occurred, the population stabilized, was far less in number than it had been BNE but would grow in time. Trucking and train deliveries began to be regular and food supplies as well as supplies of other necessities stabilized.

And the last question I will ask you, those of you who didn't live this, who didn't know the war, the killing, the horror of watching women be raped when you knew there was nothing you could do to stop it, is how do you get over it? How do you learn to be a person again, not a killing machine.

We, my dad, my friend Allan and I, or friends Jim and Dan, or many others who remain unnamed in this tale of life, how do we get over it? How do we forget? Do we give up arms? Do we give up the systems that have protected us? Do we learn to live in peace once again and exactly what does that word peace mean in our world?

For now we remain ready to fight. For now we are willing and able to defend our state, our county, our country, our home, our fortress, each other, to the end. If we have to do so again we will defend those things in a way which as it already has, will consume many more human lives. We have done those things necessary to defend ourselves in the past. If we are called upon again to defend ourselves we know how to do so in spades. If ever the flag Don't Tread on Me applied to any group of people it applies to us. That would be me Will de Young, my dad, my mother, my wife, my two sons and my friends and extended family like Allan Coxey, his wife and children. We are the survivors, the remainder of human kind in this country. We can do. We will do. But now, now we are friends to the world. Come and see us, come and be with us, come and learn about freedom, about the United States of America and its people, especially about the U.S. Marines.

RECON! HOORAW!

About the Author

Berk Rourke was born in Douglas, Arizona on August 28, 1938. His careers were in teaching 8th and 9th grade students initially and then as an attorney for a total of some 40 years. He began writing as a cathartic exercise and enjoyed it so much that he continued with multiple efforts now being published for the first time. His life has known very few limits and his writing in at least two genres now has not known limits yet. Give it a look.

* * *

To learn more about H. Berkeley Rourke and discover more Next Chapter authors, visit our website at www.nextchapter.pub.

2024
ISBN: 978-4-82411-624-6

Published by
Next Chapter
1-60-20 Minami-Otsuka
170-0005 Toshima-Ku, Tokyo
+818035793528
16th December 2021